GHOSTS

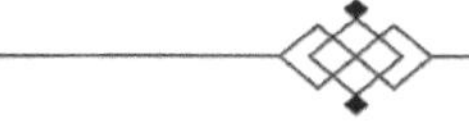

DAVID IMRIE

This international first edition published by
Divers Novels in 2024.
www.diversnovels.com

1

ISBN   978-84-09-64282-3

ISNI   0000 0005 1434 2076

<u>AI transparency</u>
This book is 100% human-written and human-edited.
Artwork uses human-edited AI-generated images.

Cover by studioannadahlberg.com

Typeset in Baskerville 11pt.

Prologue

I'm not going to make it.

I'm not going to make it back.

I should never have tried journeying so far away.

I know my strength has been fading lately. Grandma told me years ago and I should have listened: my kind don't live half as long.

I summon desperate memories.

Thomas; he was just two when he spelled 'DADDY' with his blocks; if he knows I'm coming home he goes on his old 1950s tricycle right to the far edge of the village to wait; his little, eager, keen-as-a-knife face.

God I hope, hope, hope he's not like me.

Alice, my dearest Alice, who I've still never dared tell what I can do because she'd bawl me out for the sheer waste of ability.

The house in the countryside we scraped together the money for. That chance to make a new start far away from all of this.

But it's not enough.

I'm not going to make it.

Already my capacity to care, to feel, is like paper burnt to smoke on the wind.

Hold on! Hold on for heaven's sake!

I have gold for them. So obvious; it makes sense of everything, but their wrong assumptions have prevented them from seeing it. Hughes is obsessed; I'm only out here tonight because he pushed so hard. But it means he'll pay ten times, twenty times the normal for this nugget. Enough to get me out of this damned business for good.

If I can just make it back.

And yet my will to take another step is gone.

Why hold this miserable form any longer? This shadow of my lump of flesh and bone. It's failed all it loved.

Everything is grey and unappealing.

But I can let go.

It's how to be free.

I sink to the pavement. The East End street is crowded, but of course no-one notices me lying here.

Awareness of my surroundings fades, and it's only relief.

Why did I ever even try?

No, it's better this way.

Such a burden, a mortal life.

So I release myself from it.

Ahhhh...

1.

"That's it, quiet now. Just let sleep come," Mother used to whisper in those empty evenings after Dad had gone. Its arrival always eluded me though. Instead I would be starting to drift, and next thing I knew I would awake with a head full of fading dreams. Such a loss of control infuriated me.

But then one night I caught it. My waking mind spotted the transition from a little outside myself, because that's where I'd taken to being. In that instant there was some changing of the guards, and it occurred to me that the cunning captive might escape.

Not that my body was a prison. No, I'm fond of it and it serves me decently, but bodies are so observable and dense-yet-fragile, and I desired to be otherwise.

I practiced nightly and was soon able to become apart at will. I revelled in achieving distance. I moved my existence to a thumb, the tip of a toe. Then I broke bodily contact altogether.

Instantly I was scared. This might be how you died. I rushed back from the foot of the bed into my corpse, but it was breathing away, heart still beating. It had done with me and the world for the day, recumbent and recovering its energies, and was none the wiser.

I suppose I'd hoped Dad might be there in the shadow world, waiting for me and watching over me. He wasn't, but I was used to swallowing mortality's bitter medicine by now. Instead I focused on something that, from the comics I read, I did know about: super-powers. I was eager to explore mine.

Leaving the room - moving out of sight of my physical self - was the most daunting step, but I grew calm about taking it. Despite having abandoned my eyes and ears I could see and hear. As I moved through the hall I noticed I didn't reflect in the mirror. I had achieved invisibility.

In 1982, on the night of my ninth birthday, I contrived a secret mission that would take me out of the house. I would travel the fifty or so feet across the road to the village Post Office and shop and finally get up close to the shelf of sweets behind the counter. I would not take anything of course. I was an honest-enough child, but more pertinently, in this state I could not interact with objects, merely perceive them.

I left our red-brick house via the wood of the door - passing through solids remains to this day an odd experience - and entered the shop through its glass window. It was strange being here without old Mrs. Jones' beady eye tracking me. It was exhilarating in a way. I crossed the threshold of countertop and rose to the sweet jars to float right inside amongst those sugared forms.

And yet the experience was also sterile and anticlimactic. Somehow it was devoid of joy without my body and its insatiable craving for sweetness. I persevered onwards, trying the chocolate bars: Marathon and Mars, Yorkies, Crunchies and Drifters, each bigger and unhealthier than Mother would allow me in any one sitting. All novelty was wearing off now and I was increasingly disillusioned, so I decided to curtail my excursion at the tubes of Rolos, my personal favourite. It was as I took one last shot at merging with their chocolate-and-caramel essence that I noticed one packet was different: the inside wrapper had writing on it. I didn't know why, nor even how I knew this, but it was the second packet from the right.

I formed a new, more exciting plan. This one required my body, so that was where I returned.

The next morning, a Saturday, I was awake early. I wheedled permission to buy chocolate, and, flush with a handful of coins, was outside waiting as Mrs. Jones opened the shop bang on nine.

"Been your birthday then has it, young Thomas?" she asked, eyeing the two-shilling-that-was-also-ten-new-pence piece I was brandishing.

"Yes Mrs. Jones. I'm nine now. Can I buy a packet of Rolos please?"

"Nine eh? Well course you can. 'Ere you go."

"Not that one!" I squeaked. "Could I have the second from the right one?"

She sighed in the way of people for whom all is onerous, but moved her hand.

"No, my right. Your left that would be."

"Make up your mind then," she complained, rolling her eyes, but she was now holding the packet I wanted.

I paid, returned home, and rushed to the kitchen table to unwrap the Rolos with trembling hands.

The words were there!

I squawked, causing Mother to bustle over. She commandeered the foil and read out what was printed on it: the Rowntree company, upon receipt of this lucky wrapper, of which there were only a dozen in all of Great Britain, would present me with a brand new Raleigh Chopper bicycle. There was much joyful delirium and saluting of my good fortune.

She didn't know the half of it though. My talent was proven as no dream. I truly could walk in the spirit land. Through doors and windows and walls and into even the most heavily-guarded fortress evading all detection.

How would I use it, I pondered? How would it bring me fortune, fame, my heart's desires?

And that, in the twenty-one years since, is the question I've never managed to answer.

My trick of perceiving anything written by contact alone has found me a few winning lottery scratchcards, but it transpires there aren't many out there worth serious money and you often have to buy twenty or more worthless predecessors so barely come out ahead.

If I could see the future that would make things easy, but all my ability opens up for me is secrets. Doubtless some of the financially-savvy types I studied alongside at Oxford could find lucrative angles to work, but any scheme I've ever dreamed up has quickly hit the buffers of practicality, immorality or illegality, and scared me off.

I suppose science would want to know what I can do, but to what end for me? Become a lab-rat for clinicians eager to dissect my brain? Find myself abducted to a 'secure facility' by the CIA? No thank you! For a time, as a schoolboy, I imagined myself spying for England; as an adult, though, I have to say I harbour too many doubts about England's character and motives.

Could I have gone public instead? A magic act: The Amazing Thomas Harrison will name your card or duplicate your drawing? Perhaps I could have been famous and rich that way, except the entertainment industry is full of people who are either similarly talented or very clever charlatans, and what they possess that I don't is showmanship.

No, I've been wise never to tell a single soul what I can do. My preference has always been to tuck myself away into a quiet corner and immerse myself in a book. This is probably why I read English Literature and became a writer, shunning real life choices in favour of imaginary ones.

Could my ability help me find success in this profession? For now can we just say I did explore that, but it's a double-edged sword.

Best leave it at that, if you don't mind.

How to distract from this sudden moment of awkwardness? Love; everyone likes love. Am I lucky in love? I must at least be well-informed enough to stay ahead in the game, no?

Ish, I suppose. The problem is that the search for a soul mate is a nerve-shredding thing and I have easy recourse to espionage...but, well, that's already breaking the whole covenant, isn't it? One also tends to find out things one would rather not. For instance:

'Methinks. Got to. Mescribbles! Best way! Tall and gangly, but handsome, like that one who died out of Monty Python. He's so intellectual-looking, always brownish hair tousled and blue-eyed gaze faraway above that patrician nose. Maybe he should smoke a pipe or something, if that wasn't so foul. Then he might fit together and not always be otherworldly and slightly ill-at-ease. But no: he does have this musty, academic charm which is actually quite endearing...or was at first.

Yet and yet and yet; detached, absent, elsewhere are the words which stick. He's just gone a lot, even when he's right there. So much of what he does is only going through the motions expected by those around him. He has no real Earthly passion of his own. That's it!! He knows no great reason to seize and hold every ounce of life.

But what if he ever found this? If it wasn't me - and clearly it isn't or I'd know - then would I even matter? I fear not. No, white page upon which a crystal tear might fall, I fear not.

So I can't trust him...and unfortunately there's never any getting past THAT, is there? Which equals going to have to have The Conversation, aren't I Dear Diary. Ohhh and ohh, and woe and woe. Mesighs.'

An extract from the pretentious secret journal of my ex-girlfriend. I managed the small and vicious satisfaction of breaking up with her first, but it was cold comfort because I'd liked her and thought she liked me too.

So, three years into this twenty-first century and recently

turned thirty, I'm not famous and I have no fortune. I don't even know what or who my heart's desire might be. Only that I'm as far from it as ever, save perhaps for when I was nine and for a fleeting while it was a fortuitous bicycle from a chocolate company.

A body I may possess, but what's in charge of it is passionless. The ex- was right. I think it's because I can escape, so I do escape, and so it's harder to ever truly engage.

I'm grey and insubstantial.

I'm a ghost.

Which is ironic...

2.

...Running clear, holding the tiny life with its fast-beating little heart tight against his sweating, six-packed torso, he made it out just as the upper floor crashed to the ground. Only inches behind him Biblical flames spewed through the doorframe and windows, shooting a swarm of sparks out into the night sky.

"Frank Geyser..." came the tough bark of the shadowy figure standing watching the whole shebang.

Big Len. Of course. Nothing happens in the East End that Big Len doesn't know about first, remember? His bomber jacket glinted like prescient coal in the firelight, but his eyes were dark as ocean whirlpools beneath a starless sky.

"...I cannot believe you went back in there. For a dog!"

Frank straightened, gulping in breath. "I 'ad to Len. You know 'ow Rosie feels 'bout this little fella."

There was a long pause. Crackles and pops from the burning building. Distant sirens, the fuzz coming to trample around in their size twelves.

"And 'ow, exactly, is it you feel about my Rosie, Frank?" The question was spoken with the menace of a missile

launcher's swivel.

Say it! Go on!!!

"I love 'er Len. Always 'ave. Since the second I laid eyes on 'er."

There! Done!! Would he wind up in The Thames with chains round his ankles for daring to feel this way about the gangland kingpin's daughter?

Big Len's jaws pummelled gum. Finally he growled, "Geyser. I've always wondered 'bout the name. Polack is it?"

"That's right Len." Frank drew himself tall with a pride he would never disown. "My grandad come over in thirty-nine to join the RAF. Fought in The Battle of Britain..."

"'Eroes every man wot took to them skies," put in Len.

"...then 'e fell for an English nurse while 'e were laid up recovering from a shrapnel wound, an' never went 'ome."

Len was nodding. "An' Rosie loves you too, does she?"

"I think so. I 'ope so. Sir."

"You'd treat 'er right would you?...Nah" Big Len's sudden laugh was like the staccato crackle of fireworks on Bonfire Night. "Bang out of order askin' that when you've just risked your 'ide to save that pup of 'ers, now ain't it? I've 'ad my eye on you for a while, an' you've passed all the tests. You've got my blessing, Frank Geyser."

Frank's legs were as well-muscled as a professional footballer's, but they were like jelly as he shook Big Len's suddenly-extended hand. Finally he and Rosie could drop all the secrecy and come clean to the world. It was going to be perfect. As he thought this the little dog squirmed to be put down and Frank placed it gently on the grimy tarmac. Yapping happily, it ran towards the curvaceous figure on stilettos approaching them, her golden perm glowing like a halo in the Shoreditch streetlight. "Muffin!" she cried out, and knelt to smother the puppy with kisses.

Big Len was looking at him, his eyes now twinkling with the amusement of a young boy with a pocket full of pennies at a fairground. "Well go on then. Go to 'er. You go on, my son."

'My son'! Big Len had called him 'my son'!! Frank Geyser nodded respectfully to his future father-in-law, then kept it down to a manly stride over to the love of his life.

He'd finally been accepted into East End royalty, and he wasn't going to let no-one down.

Not now.

Not never.

The End...for now!!
Frank Geyser will return in [TBD: title]

O sweet bejesus how I nauseate myself.

Still, it wraps book five of the series, in which Frank Geyser achieves his legitimisation. Shinelle, for whom I'm paid decently to write this simile-fest drivel, will be delighted.

Tarquin will too, even though he seemed a little off his usual assured game the other day. I'm not sure why, since he knows I produce reliably.

As agents are always cheered by a completed manuscript, especially one almost a week ahead of schedule, I decide to share the happy news with him right away. I call his office but his secretary says he's out and about. I try his mobile. It rings and rings. I let it, because I've seen him trying to work one.

"Thomas?" From the background noise he's on a busy street somewhere. His voice sounds strained. I can picture him: immaculately turned out by his family tailor, six inches taller than everyone around him and staring furrow-browed over their heads in that upper-class bafflement everyone mistakes for profundity. "Look, I was rather hoping you wouldn't get wind of things, but all is not a lost cause."

That slaps the dozy smile right off my face. "Wind of what things, Tarq?"

"Ah. Eh? Oh, minor things. Piffling. For another time. Over coffee perhaps? New Swedish place almost next door. Supposed to be interesting. How ARE we Tom? What news?"

I could call him out, but my natural tendency is to play the game. "Good. Very good. Frank Geyser just got his Rosie and the manuscript's ready to send on to Shinelle. In fact if the brief's there for the next instalment I can keep right on going, now I'm in character and whatnot."

"Super. Super! Would that all writers could turn the handle like you do Tom. Wonderful. But best to give Frank a little time off though. At least until after we've met The Witch."

"The Witch? Is she coming to London?" The Witch is Robyn Brookes from the US partner of Tarquin senior's literary agency. A visit is a rare surprise, and never a welcome one.

"Flying by, yes. Flying by and dropping in. But she did mention something about recent developments she needed to share. Calling you was literally next on my to-do list. Listen, can you pop over to Southwark tomorrow? The Witch is due at noon, thus a brew at eleven-thirty? Cover a spot of preamble?"

I say okay. What else can I say? Etonians learn to hide all feelings aged eight so I'm not going to winkle anything out of him sooner. Wind of what? The Witch? I don't like this. I don't like it one bit. Urgency in the literary world always goes hand-in-hand with some tension. Damn it, what can it be?!

An annoying byproduct of being able to find out secrets like I do is that you hate the ones hidden from you more.

3.

I take the tube to Bond Street then the Jubilee Line south

across the river to the new station at Southwark. Cafes are springing up around it, and I find 'Mork & Stark of Stockholm' as per Tarquin's secretary's instructions. I'm on time. He's not here.

Inside it's quiet, all birch cleanliness and alcoves, Scandinavian pastries and coffee smell. I'm hoping for the attractive blonde waitress but instead I draw the guy who looks like a yeti. "Hey," he booms. "I'm Anders. What can I fix you up with?"

"Just a coffee please."

"Yeah sure, but, like, what kind?"

He passes me a menu but none of it means anything to me, so I tell him something to keep me alert at an important meeting, with milk, then Tarquin crashes in.

"Apologies, apologies," he says to me. "Two of, please," to Anders, in a welter of gesticulation.

"I've been on tenterhooks all night Tarq. Why is The Witch here, and why on Earth does she want to see a lowly creature like me?"

He has a long, bendy face, and it contorts into a grimace. "Not quite sure, to tell you the truth. Word is there's some big authenticity issue with Shinelle and The Witch's tour is about plugging leaks before they happen. That genre of problem."

"Meaning people have found out she uses a ghostwriter?"

He shakes his head. "Possibly, but I rather think that cat was never in the bag. Hardly uncommon after all."

"Then how do I come into things?"

"Well, as said pen-wielding sprite a degree of involvement is inevitable, but I only really know what I already told you. And that The Witch has been in discussions with legal. All they'll say to me is 'situation containment'."

Both of us have to wait while Anders delivers our coffees and tells us interminably about an artisan grower community in deepest Ethiopia. "Enjoy!" he shouts, finally going. He's also left the bill: Costly Coffee they should call this place.

"Okay Tarq, but then why all the ominous 'wind of things' stuff yesterday?"

"Um." Why does he look so damned gloomy? "Oh, all right, but this is hush-hush and you didn't hear it from me. Thing is I happened to be at the publishers about another book, and as they were pulling that up on the computer I got a glance at the overview screen for our agency...and, er, I'm pretty sure the status for the Geyser book five you just finished was 'under review'."

"What?! But it already has a release date."

"Well quite." He sips his coffee, one eyelid twitching.

"Tarq, Geyser's my bread and butter. You remember I just bought the flat in Notting Hill? My mortgage payments are huge."

"I know, I know."

"But when the American TV adaptation pilot got good ratings you told me it was a banker for the long term. 'Reliable as Switzerland' were your exact words, I believe."

That mobile face falls and I already regret my unfairness. When we were at Oxford together he wanted to travel the developing world and escape his privilege doing Meaningful Things, but his father talked him into giving it a year at the agency, which turned into eight and counting. He was the one who landed me the Geyser job in the first place. Despite my history.

"I'm sorry Tarq." I mean it sincerely. "Whatever this is, I know you're in no way to blame. Nor for my financial decisions."

He manages a smile but he still looks like a dog that's been kicked. "Look, chin up. Could all be crossed wires. Let's see what The Witch says. Just wanted to give you a heads up."

"I really appreciate it. All that you do for me in fact." I take a long pull of my coffee. It's good, but also bitter and dark. I feel it descend into the already-churning pit of my stomach.

"Tarquin, Thomas, my two favourite tall English gents. How is your country so bad at basketball?" Robyn's voice is chipper and she winks at her own joke. She's got that Human Resources impregnable façade. We fold ourselves into meeting room chairs and wait like schoolboys.

"So, so, so. Now the reason I wanted to connect face-to-face is that this is kinda delicate." Two copies of a document are handed to us stiffly. I think her power suit stops her moving properly. Her forehead is equally immobile; botox no doubt. It's all very unnerving. "In fact first up I'll just need a signature on this from you both."

I'd like to take a look at the other papers which she's not sharing yet, but zoning out wouldn't exactly be a sensible move. What she's given us is a confidentiality agreement. A vague and seemingly Draconian one, although I'm no legal expert. I sign mine because there's no indication I have any real choice in the matter. I notice that for a literary agent Tarquin is a surprisingly slow reader. Robyn and I sit frozen until he's finished and has also signed. Even as she collects the two papers her whole demeanour hardens.

"Ooookay then. Now Robyn's a real busy girl on this trip across the pond so I'm going to get right into it. It turns out Shinelle has what we're terming 'an Ali G problem'."

Tarquin and I look nonplussed, and the extreme edges of Robyn's forehead try to frown. "Meaning she's not what she claims to be."

Again we have no idea how to respond, and we're now two class dunces with an increasingly irate teacher. She resorts to sarcasm. "So you do remember Shinelle Grimes, right? Inspiring mixed-race immigrants' kid from some impoverished high-rise shithole in the worst bit of East London? A lifetime of social exclusion and racism and police brutality and drugs and crime all around, and yet the novelist buried deep inside her soul shines through and she creates the bestselling Frank Geyser series which we're the agents for? You're familiar with that?"

"Yes," we mumble.

"Well hoorah! Except now the Saturday night talk show preppers do their due diligence for the TV tie-in and it turns out that's not her real background at all."

"You thought it was?" I answer, before realising the stupidity of doing so.

"You knew it wasn't?" She glares at Tarquin and I in turn.

"I'd no idea." He shrugs awkwardly.

"I mean it's pretty obvious she's middle-class and putting on an act." I also shrug.

"And how, pray, is that pretty obvious, Mister Harrison?"

"Well, the accent has inconsistencies for a start. And then her cultural and linguistic references don't particularly suggest an East End upbringing, or anything close."

"Jesus fucking Christ! Fucking Brits! Fucking hell! And no-one ever thought to - hello - mention that she wasn't the genuine article?!"

Tarquin's squirming under the tirade, and I feel unjustly stung. "To be fair, that is hinted at by her not actually writing her own books. I do that," I say mildly.

The Witch's eyes narrow, and now I'm wishing I'd refrained from the smart-arse retort, complete with its unnecessary and provocative 'actually'. It's that wretched Swedish coffee; my heart's thumping crazily and every muscle in my torso feels like it's on the verge of spasm.

"Yes Thomas, you do write the books. At least to date. And of course if anyone should be able to spot a fraud it's you, isn't it? But in fact that's a nice segue into why we need this meeting. Thank you. So we're doing damage limitation with the publisher, and the headline is that book five is on ice for now. You'll still be paid the base fee of course, but sales percentage only if it ever sees the light of day. The retainer stays in force for two more years and means you have to provide books six through eight if we ask for them. And if we decide you're the best writer for them. At the moment, however, further work on any Geyser title is not authorised to proceed."

It's turned inky and raining outside the meeting room window. I catch my reflection in it. I'm gaping like a landed fish.

"So thanks for now Thomas. We're all super-appreciative of your efforts here." The Human Resources smile is back and I wonder if I somehow dreamed the last couple of minutes. "If you don't mind I just need a moment alone with Tarquin."

I rise docilely to my feet and walk out and down the hall to the seating area, where I pick a chair with my back to the receptionist. The Witch has followed far enough to make sure I don't linger and try to eavesdrop. Good. That buys me some precious extra seconds.

I fold my body's arms and close its eyes, and soon I'm out of it and back through the closed door and into the meeting room. Tarquin's reading the second document, a bullet-pointed list with my name near the top.

"Is this really necessary? Tom has done sterling work for us and none of this is his fault."

"I understand that you were friends, Tarquin, but we need you to think like an agent. Even as we speak all this is hitting the fan. How far's it gonna spread? We need separation here. I like that you had no idea about Shinelle. That's good. That's the line to take. We're innocent victims of her deceit, just like everyone else. But what we must not have getting out is that we set up a ghostwriter for her. And what cannot ever be allowed anywhere near the public domain is that that writer was Thomas Harrison. You know why he's toxic, and you must see how his history and this Shinelle mess could join up into a perfect shitstorm so big it sinks the whole agency?"

Tarquin shakes his head. "I don't know how you do things over in New York, but we don't abandon a chap this way. Father won't agree."

The Witch just looks at him. I think if her face were capable of expression its current one might be pity. "These are your father's orders. All contact ceases today. No-one so much as mentions Thomas' name here. We exorcise him."

4.

I have a nasty déjà vu to the ex's diary when Tarquin emerges and I know the secret. His face is tense and mournful, the way he gets over injured pigeons in the street.

"Better not here," he mutters, forestalling my questions. I follow him out of the building, a little way down the road and into the first café we pass.

It's the Swedish one and I pause at the door. "Do we want to come back to this place? It's kind of pricey." I'm suddenly very aware of money.

"On me," he murmurs, and we continue in and sit. At least the place is private; we're almost the only ones here. The blonde waitress and Anders the yeti are having a hushed argument at the till, so we're left in peace.

"Look Tom, no easy way to say this."

I try to look like I think I should look if I didn't already know what The Witch told him. You'd imagine I'd be a better actor than this by now, but no.

"Shinelle is very damaged goods for the mo' and The Witch wants you clear of the danger zone in case of enquiries."

"Meaning what exactly, Tarq?"

He sighs. "Agency can't represent you and you don't tell anyone you've worked for us. Sorry."

"And they expect me to just go along with that?!"

This is torturing Tarquin, but it's that or find a way to admit I was there when she explained it all.

"Afraid it's buried in the contract you signed back there. Dirty trick. Not my doing. Please believe me Tom."

Finally I can relent. "I know that Tarq. So why did she make you sign one too?"

"Just as cover I think. Don't know. Didn't grasp all the legalese properly."

"Who does? But is this really it? Just goodbye and good luck, oh and don't ever mention our name?" It's hitting me again as I say it. Also that money side. I've got savings to hold out maybe three or four weeks, then direct debits start bouncing.

"There's nothing I can do."

If we were Italian this tension would call for shouting or hugging, but we're English and distance and decorum must be maintained. I suspect the resulting ache of isolation is why our nation produces such great writers. I resolve to at least not drag Tarquin down with me.

"Tarq it's fine. Listen, you've been a firm friend throughout, and I know none of this can be laid at your door. You do all you need to do, and we're okay. But if you've got any suggestions on where I go from here then, well, I would love to hear them."

"Because I'm such a dashed good agent?" Now his face is creased with self-loathing, another of Albion's beastly specialities.

I dredge up a smile from somewhere. "In that you have no talent for lying and aren't much motivated by money? I'm asking as a friend Tarq, that's all." A relationship even The Witch's contract cannot explicitly prohibit, although his father will doubtless be laying down some laws soon enough.

He attempts a forlorn smile back, then turns serious. "If you need something to pay the bills and soon, then all I can suggest is Danny Decker. He was keen as mustard to get you after you did Sid's book. Far as I know he's never engaged anyone else."

"No way! Not that Tarq. Not all that again." I mean this more than I've meant anything in a long while.

"Look Tom, thing is you've specialised as an East End crime writer..."

"Completely by accident!"

"But nonetheless. And that genre is on the wane. People don't want gangsters anymore. They're decorating their way up the property ladder with Kirsty and Phil, and jaunty criminals with all their casual destruction no longer amuse. They want wizards and elves. Escapism. Danny's a last chance to milk it while you regroup. A way to put a roof over one's head."

Says the man whose family haven't been on the wrong end of a mortgage in a dozen generations or more. "I don't think you get how unpleasant a character Sid Marsh was, Tarq. And why would you? I hid it all behind down-to-Earth humour, family loyalty and fake East End bonhomie in his autobiography. I cleansed him with all the word power I could muster, and it's something I regret quite bitterly. But now you want me to do the same for his by-all-accounts nastier protégé?"

"Didn't say I wanted that, did I Tom? And you'll remember I let it drop three years ago despite the sizeable amount being offered. Got something of a tongue-lashing from Father in fact. You asked as a friend. All I can think of."

He's right and I'm wrong, and I apologise to him, even going so far as to lean forward and grasp him awkwardly by the upper arm, causing embarrassment all round. Everything possible has been said, and after a glance at his watch he takes his leave. I already know I'll go quietly, if for no other reason than to make it easier on this proven friend.

I am not doing Danny Decker's autobiography though. I will not let myself get drawn back into that world.

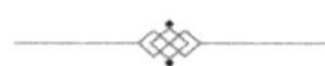

"Hey!"

I look up and it's the blonde waitress. She places a swirl bun on a small plate in front of me. I smell cinnamon. It brings me a tiny wisp of cosiness.

"I apologise so much for the delay. I am Elin. Here is a kanelbullar on the house, as you say, yes?" I love her accent. Every 's' is like sunlight in an icicle.

"Yes. Thanks. That's very kind of you."

She wants to say something else, so I force my face to look inviting.

"Forgive me if this is rude. You came back here; is it okay to ask why?"

I've been trying not to look at her too properly because she's beautiful and I don't want to gawp, but now I focus. Maybe I'm externalising, but her day seems to be going as badly as mine. "To be honest just because it's close to the office we were at. It's nice and quiet too."

The corner of her mouth twists. She can even grimace attractively. "That is the Catch-22 though."

I twig; who says literary knowledge is of no use in life? "As in if it stays this quiet there won't be any café for the people wanting to come and find quiet in?"

She nods, not happily.

"I think the problem could be a price thing," I offer. "It's nice in here but in this part of London pretty much everyone's rushing somewhere in a hurry. I suppose they just want a caffeine hit for not too much money. Oh yes, and also maybe not like the one I had earlier. It made me horribly shaky."

Now she frowns. "What did Anders recommend for you?"

"Er...It was Ethiopian I think. Artisan growers. Perhaps some sort of co-operative?"

"That is our darkest roast! Why must he always be so extreme?" She's suddenly angry. "And of course this is not coffee you are used to. What is it you normally drink? I mean at home."

"Well, NiceCaff for the most part really."

"The granules in a plastic jar?" From her reaction I might have boasted that I collect faeces and offered her a sniff.

"It's just a convenience thing. I mean I know it's not like ground coffee. It's just neater and faster. Less cleaning up."

She's not even listening anymore. "How is it people cannot see the difference? That is just every substandard, contaminated or surplus bulk crop from everywhere aggregated together in a huge, environmentally-destructive industrial process with chemicals to make it go faster than nature. There is no passion. No individuality. It is totally generic and about making money. It is only riding on the coattails of proper coffee and all its centuries of indigenous history. That muck has no story behind its taste. It is a flavour devoid of any love."

She sees my face collapse and her hand flies to her mouth. "Oh I am so, so sorry! It is just a bad day in a bad month. My brother and I were fighting again," she inclines her head towards Anders, "but I have no excuse to take this attitude with a customer. I really am so sorry. Listen, can I bring you one cup of real coffee, also on the house. Please? Just stay here five more minutes, okay?"

I nod dazedly, she rushes off, and I'm left to mull over why I reacted that way. I suppose because it's not pleasant to hear a wholly negative metaphor for yourself. Hi, I'm literary NiceCaff. Flavour-of-the-month is 'he'll give it you straight' Frank Geyser a-la-Shinelle, but I'm good for a reliable four-to-five-thousand words per day in any colour. Principles? Please, sir, we're not that sort of establishment! It's all for sale, and at a bargain price.

I did have my own stories once. I sweated over and honed them. Sent them to publishers and agencies, magazines, newspapers, anywhere. But no-one wanted them, and in time, as I re-read and re-edited in a doom-loop, I also came to see all I'd written as the trite mush it presumably always was.

But rather than quit completely I went back to the start. 'What do they seek, these agents and publishers who are the gatekeepers of the printed word? How can I better please them?' When I rewired my mind that way I turned out to have more talent. But did I disconnect my heart in the process?

Elin is back. She gingerly places a small cup in front of me. "Our parents own Sweden's largest coffee company. The family business supplies supermarkets, vending machine companies and a huge chain of furniture store restaurants. It is super-successful, and they want Anders and I to take management roles in it. But we made a deal: a small artisan roasting setup and this café in our mormor's and farmor's lost surnames. If Mork & Stark is not making a profit in eighteen months it will close and we will take their jobs. That was five months ago. And as you see..." she gestures around the café, which is now completely empty save Anders, who is watching us. "I want to know if I am wasting my time. Maybe people never will appreciate the difference. I really need to know this."

I feel like an executioner as I lift the cup to my mouth. I

know nothing about coffee. I don't even want to know things about coffee. I just want it to do its business so I can crank out... That stray thought appals me so much that when I take the first sip my mind is a blank canvas.

It's day after endless night. Colour and vibrancy and birdsong replace murky void. And the story of how is there! I taste it! The seasons; growth's marriage to decay. Nature's new gift ripened by summer, respect and reciprocation in the care of the harvesters. Sunshine itself is in here. Soil's richness. Air's purity. Blissful rain that maintains glorious life.

I look up at Elin and I swear there are almost tears in my eyes. She sees, and she claps her hands together and looks skywards.

"This is from Geisha Arabica beans. A single estate high in the mountains of Panama, sown and reaped according to the moon phase. It's a medium roast, far more appropriate for you than what my brother chose. So you understand?"

My answer is postponed by Anders' interjection. "And to make a profit we have to sell it for nine pounds per cup." Behind his beard he looks mournful. "Of the few people who do buy it no-one comes back. Elin, you know this. It is too expensive for the amount most people care. It is beyond time we faced this fact."

Both of them turn horribly to me for arbitration.

"It really is great-tasting coffee, but I just don't know. That's a lot of money. And this is London."

Anders clearly think he's won. I suppose he has. I feel like Judas. I get up to leave, pocketing Tarquin's tenner when Elin refuses to take it.

Outside in the stinking drizzle I must also face a fact: unless I want to see my life fall out of my control and apart, I don't think I have any choice: I'll have to contact Danny Decker, and sooner rather than later.

The yeti was right.

It is hard truth.

Because if that glorious sensation I just tasted is a failure, how does my quality stack up by comparison?

I may have had illusions once, but they're no longer something I can afford.

5.

I get back to Notting Hill and my flat. It's tiny and basic, but it's the toehold in the capital any committed writer needs. Even if it feels like it's causing more problems than it's solving today.

I need the clarity of detachment to make one last bid for an alternative, so I lie on the bed, I induce sleep, and I wander. This is my term for roving in ghost form away from my body.

After that youthful experiment with the sweet counter at the village Post Office, I went on to explore the how far and how long aspects of my ability. It took me some years to gain an understanding. It was also something that altered subtly as I turned adult, and it continues to do so.

The main restriction is something I call 'the sadness', and you could probably make a mathematical formula out of how it works. As soon as I separate from my body this sadness begins to build. Within half an hour or so everything starts to feel grey and unappealing, and it becomes harder and harder to find anything to care about enough to want to stay in this world. On top of this time effect is a distance multiplier. The farther I am from my mortal bones the faster the sadness grows. It may well be exponential.

When I was twenty and at Oxford I discovered my limit. Somewhat drunk after a party at which I'd failed to impress a girl I really wanted to impress, I detached, left my student digs south of the river, and hitched a ride on a night bus to the city centre. My impulse was to explore the hidden vaults of the Bodleian Library, where there was rumoured to be an underground train system.

I got to The Radcliffe Camera and made my way inside and downwards, but the sadness was claiming me rapidly. I became afraid and turned homewards, but grew slower and slower. For a time I didn't believe I would hold together long enough to get back to my body, but I made it, just, and awoke gasping, sweat-drenched and terrified.

I'd understood I could simply drift apart and disappear from this mortal life, and I'd increasingly wanted to. You might imagine it as a question of mere willpower to hold on, but ask yourself what willpower is built upon. What I touched the boundary of is, I'm sure, how the spirit dies. Worst of all was how attractive oblivion's brochure is. It caught in my head that night, and, if I'm honest, it grows ever more potent.

So this evening I daren't go near that edge, which has been feeling especially close of late, but I also need out for a while.

I slide up my wall - for reasons I don't understand, I always need to maintain contact with a solid surface; I can't fly. Nor can I walk on or in water. I know intuitively I'd come instantly apart if I tried; Ghosts definitely can't do water.

I go out through the ceiling structure above my flat, and I perch on the roof gazing absently at a West London cul-de-sac. So many lights and so many curtains. So many different-hued windows. So many different lives going on behind them. I could make my way into any one of those rooms and observe everything from inside. I could find out their secrets, their stories.

But I don't do that anymore. Not since...

Okay. Fine. You might have been wondering why The Witch called me toxic and what the various mentions of my history refer to. I alluded to it, but you probably want the facts.

That story; my story. Because stories are what all of us crave whenever and wherever we can get them, aren't they? It's the human condition. So why not? While I'm disembodied.

Eight years ago I graduated from university believing I would be at the vanguard of a new generation of writers. I imagined myself being feted and adored. For a while I lived and typed on maternal goodwill back in Dorset, but friction was building with Geoff - who Mother married when I was thirteen - so for the latter stages I relocated to a cheap rented bedsit in East London.

I guess part of me was seeking the real there. Another part was probably seeking my dad. He was from Guildford but apparently used to go on mysterious 'business trips' to the East End.

I found neither, but I did complete my debut novel and was wholly convinced by it. I sent it out widely - as you know - and sat back, waiting for the bidding war to begin.

Four months of ensuing silence was my education.

I became bitter. I reworked and lost clarity and faith and time, but still felt the idea of my not being the genuine article frighteningly impossible. Then, as I said, I refocused on the various agents and publishers who had rejected me. I sought answers I was prepared to hear, and the conclusion I came to was that I was the wrong gender, colour and class.

Please holster the flamethrower! I used the past tense. I know what you're thinking: an educated, white, middle-class male complaining that doors are closed to him? Really? Has he not noticed that his is, in fact, by far and away the demographic most-represented on bookshelves? It's true, but there was also some validity in noting that the white male authors from the 80s, 70s, 60s, 50s, and everything before back to and including Socrates and St. Paul, were still in print and badly skewing those metrics.

These dead, already-successful writers would forever remain as my live educated-white-male competition.

Whereas if you went into a bookshop and asked for a novel by a black woman many wouldn't be able to offer you a single one. Hence the desire of publishing houses to redress the imbalance, and hence my big, bright idea.

The devious spark was the last photo on a thirty-six exposure roll of film. I needed to use it up and send it off so I snapped a careless picture of the grubby Whitechapel street outside my window. It was only when I got the prints back that I saw the woman. She was still young, probably in her 20s and with a beautiful strength to her cheekbones, but you could also see that she had her ghosts. Her eyes were focused on something out of shot, and the worries of the world were written like elegant poetry across her countenance.

...which I shamelessly appropriated. Along with eavesdropped vignettes of the lives of people in flats within wandering distance. I took their world and shone my frustration upon it, with all my middle-class vocabulary and Oxford-trained technique.

Five weeks later I had a raw manuscript called "I Still See The Light", and without even stopping to think I entered it into Britain's foremost literary competition for unpublished authors. The name I used was deliberately black and female to go with that unknown woman's face, cropped out of context and enlarged. The faked biography was a cynical composite of everything I believed agents and publishers to be seeking as mitigation for their own educated, sheltered, middle-class whiteness.

I never planned for it to win.

I don't know what my plan was, truth be told. I've blotted it all from my memory as much as I'm able. Even recalling it distresses my body into a cold sweat, which is why I'm only sharing this whilst in my phantom state.

You can probably guess what happened next. When the inevitable finding out occurred and there'd already been so much publicity.

The headlines. The scandal. The pillorying.

There was a silver lining of sorts though: the episode caught the attention of the East End's self-proclaimed favourite son, Sid Marsh, who was apparently tickled pink by it. In the whole Lock, Stock and late 90s gangster craze agents were queuing up for his autobiography. Can't write for toffee? Don't worry about that, we'll arrange a ghost. Sid asked for me. Tarquin's dad suddenly remembered who I was and sent his son round to sell me on the deal. I didn't take much persuading. The book, sans all reference to my tainted name, did pretty well with both punters and critics, and I picked up the Shinelle gig off the back of it. 'Frank Geyser' was my stupid pun, by the way. Meant as a joke until they liked it seriously.

But, as Tarquin reminded me today, there was an earlier job offer I turned down. Danny Decker, Sid's notorious protégé-turned-rival. 'As Nails' was Sid's version of history, so unsurprisingly Danny didn't come out of it well. I guess he wanted his reply using the same voice, because he kept on asking. Even the impressive fee wasn't enough to tempt me though. My single foray into that world had been too much. I was petrified throughout every interview with Sid and each time I handed in a draft chapter. I was desperate to get back to the safe havens of pure fiction.

And in Geyser I thought I'd found myself a harbour there, but no more it seems.

So now you're caught up with me, and with not even the whiff of an alternative occurring to me up here, I must once again get caught up in what I thought I'd escaped.

My fear hasn't lessened, but I'll make the call to Danny's

people in the morning.

For now I need to hasten back to my body.

The sadness is getting too much.

6.

Because I was so keen never to use it, I still remember the contact information from three years ago. 'The Topaz Table nightclub. Ask for Maureen'. I look it up in the phone book, take a deep breath, and dial.

"Topaz Table." It's a man's voice. Someone who was up late the night before, and a lot of nights prior to that.

"Good morning. Can I speak to Maureen please?"

"'Oo is this?"

"My name's Thomas Harrison. I'm calling about a request Mr. Decker made some while ago."

There's no reply but I hear footsteps and distant murmuring. High heels clack closer.

"Hello Mr. Harrison. This is Maureen." Her accent is still East End, but barely. Sid wouldn't have trusted it.

"Good morning. I'm not sure if you'll recall this, but three years ago you were in contact with the Pevensey Literary Agency about Mr. Decker's autobiography, and he was asking specifically for me."

There's a pause. "Yes, I remember. You're the one who wrote Sid's book for him."

"Yes." Technically this reply is breach of contract, but Sid lives in sunny Spain now and the unsold copies of 'As Nails' have long since been consigned to the bargain bins or pulped.

"Mr. Decker made a very generous offer which you turned down, isn't that correct?"

It's no surprise they're going to stick the knife in a bit. If there are two words that capture the essence of autobiography they are ego and grudge. Also these particular people are better than you want to know about with knives.

"At the time I'd just finished Sid's book and I was worried about having to be both sides' voices in a public argument." It's my rehearsed excuse.

"I see. But now things have changed?"

"Time has passed and water has flowed under the bridge. I feel there would no longer be any conflict of interests in my working with Mr. Decker. That's if he's still interested of course. I'm merely enquiring."

"I'll discuss this with Mr. Decker and get back to you. This is still via Pevensey I assume?"

"No, it's direct."

There's no way to tell on a phone, but I'm sure she's raising an eyebrow. She must also understand who holds the cards now. "Can you give me a contact number?"

I tell her and she rings off. Yesterday I swore blind I didn't want this job and now I'm on tenterhooks that I won't get it.

Life; it's depressingly absurd.

Maureen calls back the next morning. "Mr. Decker will see you in person. Nine-o-clock at The Topaz Table."

"Is that nine p.m.?" I realise it's an idiotic question even as I ask it. I'm a morning writer by preference, but things turn nocturnal on that side of London.

"Yes. Tonight. Come round to the side door on Odiham Crescent."

"I'll be there. Please thank Mr. Decker for making the time."

"Mm-hm," and the line goes dead.

So this is it; back into the terrible fray. I gaze wistfully at my desk by the window with its neatly arranged computer and notebooks. I may have known Shinelle was a fraud from the moment I met her, but she left me alone here to get on with the writing. We had a good devil's bargain. If I do manage to agree this next one, it's going to be a lot less cosy.

Everything gets gradually grittier and grimmer as I clank eastwards in a graffiti-tagged carriage on the Docklands Light Railway. It reflects my thoughts too well.

Everything is the wrong way around. Had I considered Danny's offer three years ago I would have been the expert, the one deciding. He would have had to show me his story, convince me of its worth. Now I'm a beggar for his money and whether there's narrative value is irrelevant.

But in the end that's just supply and demand, isn't it? Money and the balance of power. Therefore life's price is agree the fee, do the job, and keep meeting my mortgage payment schedule.

But maybe Danny will possess a good story after all.

I have, in fact, always been curious. He had no family and little more than the clothes he stood up in when Sid met him. He'd been climbing the ranks as a bareknuckle boxer, but a detached retina put paid to that at twenty-two. Sid, who of course had his juicy cut from the bouts, took pity on him and gave him some odd jobs. Danny's controlled violence as an enforcer had just the right amount of astuteness and inconsistency. He was also diligent and unusually intelligent, and he rapidly did well.

Reading between the lines - obviously, because Sid never outright confirmed anything which might risk prosecution - Danny's six months At Her Majesty's Pleasure in 1968 were in place of one of Sid's lieutenants. That earned him his East End badge of honour. Even so, after that he seemed to either find his level or keep his distance, because for the next six years he was largely peripheral. Then, in 1975, some change took him. If there's a story then that's where it resides: when Danny suddenly morphed into the cold-eyed-yet-suave hardcase profiteer of popular infamy, rising meteorically to become Sid's second-in-command.

Was it falling in love with Sid's only child, his daughter Bella, that made the difference? I know Danny pleaded for Sid's blessing, because Sid told me so more than once. It was given, but I'm not sure how willingly, as Sid would instantly turn ice cold if I tried to delve there. The marriage was in 1976, but it didn't last long. In 1979 Bella died at just twenty-five years old. No-one seems to know what of or why, but after it happened the two men never spoke again.

Danny Decker had become a big player in the East End by that time, so he could diverge from his mentor and retain an empire. As the ethos of greed replaced that of gentlemen-only-greed, and 1980s London opened up to blood of any colour, his reach and wealth grew rapidly. Sid's, meanwhile, showed its age, turning brittle and withered.

Sid didn't have me call Danny an ungrateful traitor to both him and the East End in general, but he was happiest when that was the insinuation in the writing I produced. In the half-chances that arose to broach the relationship with him, I always got the impression that Danny had been trusted with the most precious thing of all, and Danny had failed.

And yet the picture has to be more complex than that. If Sid believed Danny was responsible, even through simple negligence, for his beloved Bella's death, then it would have been war instead of careful tiptoeing round each other...

Unless, that is, Danny had some iron hold over Sid.

I'm shocked that this has never occurred to me until now, because it makes a lot of irritating loose ends click into place.

And what better hold could there be than knowing the truth about the slayings of Terry 'Nosey' Norris and Detective Constable Brian Hughes?

It's one of the great unsolved East End mysteries. Tarquin senior was most keen that I ferret about it when interviewing Sid, but I quickly realised that it would be taking my life in my hands to do so.

Or at least to do so corporeally. Of course I was curious. And I did manage to employ my hidden talent to investigate...but it would have been the height of suicidal idiocy to let what I discovered get anywhere near Sid or his book.

We shudder to a halt, I alight to the platform, and with one last check of my London A-to-Z I set off into the orange-lit murk towards The Topaz Table.

The side door opens before I even have time to knock, and a muscular, unspeaking guy takes me in through a labyrinth of dimly-lit rooms where preparations for the night's work are underway. Two ladies in sequins giggle at me through an open door, and somewhere a husky-voiced singer is warming up. We climb a flight of stairs. He knocks once at a door, opens it, and nods me inside.

What does one expect of a gangster's lair? Not a spacious office with what look like Danish designer lamps and chairs. I take the seat that's waiting for me opposite the woman at the conference table.

"Welcome to The Topaz Table, Mr. Harrison," says Maureen, whose voice I recognise. And the table does indeed appear to be inset with topaz in a whole range of hues running through blue, yellow and orangey-brown to red and diamond-clear. It must have cost an absolute fortune. "I'll just go through a couple of preliminaries with you before Mr. Decker arrives."

There's a weighty non-disclosure agreement, which Maureen explains to me, managing to imply bodily consequences for breach without ever being explicit. And I'm being paid one hundred pounds for this meeting, which is useful for me and also for them, since it binds a contract. I sign it all and pocket the two crisp fifty-pound-notes.

Having stood in gentlemanly fashion as Maureen left, I move over to the bookshelf once I'm alone. It covers all of one wall and is dominated by history books; Kings, religions, battles and successions. Also tomes on philosophy, politics, modern finance and strategic warfare.

Sid's voice comes back to me now, out in his garden, where I'd try and steer him to avoid the cigarette stink. "Left school at fourteen without an exam to 'is name an' 'ad on chip on 'is shoulder about it ever since, our Danny. Elocution lessons 'e got 'isself. Elocution lessons! Well I guess 'e's done alright out of 'obnobbin' with MPs an' them art world an' lit'ry types an' whatnot, but if 'e'd of tried any o' them airs an' graces when 'e worked for me 'e'd of got a clip round the ear to remind 'im where 'e come from an' no fuckin' mistake."

Of course everything Sid said about Danny was bile-tinged, but there's a way to tell whether it's pseudo-intellectualism. I bend closer. A decent number of the spines do in fact have creases. This isn't just for show.

"So?"

I didn't even hear him enter, and I jump. Straight away that fear I felt with Sid is back in the pit of my stomach. The knowledge that I'm closeted with a man who could kill, would kill, and very probably has killed.

Danny Decker is average height and trim, and you'd guess him at late forties rather than his actual fifty-eight years. He holds himself like a younger man, but there's also some expensive grooming to his facade; the salt and pepper hair has more pepper skilfully worked in; the nose that was bent sideways in the sixties retains its history of being broken, but now has a sculpted look and breathes silently. He projects authority of the kind that bites instantly and hard if provoked. Money, but not the uniformed conformity of The City. The grey trousers and black roll-neck jumper are highest quality, Italian probably. No rings, no watch. The titanium-rimmed glasses reflect just enough to cloak the eyes and what are surely deep fatigue lines around them.

And it's the eyes that have it. There IS a story here, I'm weirdly sure of it now. But shielded by something as layered and liable to make you cry as an onion.

"Mr. Decker, it's..."

"Danny. I don't stand on ceremony. You were saying?" His English has, as Sid complained, been assiduously tutored away from its natural form.

"Danny, it's precisely not for me to say. I'm a hired set of skills that can construct a book, but the content's all you."

He considers the implications of this. "So Sid's as embittered and stuck-in-the-past as he comes across in 'As Nails'?"

I take my time before answering too. "For me, that would be an oversimplification."

He smiles, although that's a borderline verb for displaying teeth that way. "I like that when you take someone's money you stay loyal. Are you capable of discarding all you've heard about me from Sid, though?"

"Yes, I am."

"And do you want to write this book, Thomas? Frank Geyser does strike me as mostly about making rent. Or should I say mortgage."

How the hell does he know about Geyser and my flat? "I'll do a professional job either way," I reply a little stiffly. "But I prefer it if there's a story to tell. The readers and critics will like that better too."

He studies me expressionlessly. "Alright then. We'll start on Monday. Maureen will give you the details."

We shake hands, his grip dry and firm, and then he's gone as swiftly as he entered. I'm left to reflect on a man who isn't only the worm-turned-snake Sid would have you believe.

What is he then? I can mimic Tarquin's upper-class mannerisms well enough, but the giveaway is my lack of knowing nothing else. It's the curse of the chameleon, and I recognise it in Danny Decker, whose true colours remain entirely unclear to me.

Strangest of all, though, is his obvious reluctance. That's the one sentiment never normally encountered in autobiography. He wanted to show me who was boss, and yet my clear impression was that he was being forced into this. By whom, how, and why?

Maureen comes back in moments later and places a contract on the table. My eyes jump straight to the fee. It's twenty percent more than I was offered three years ago, and I let my surprise show.

"Given your lack of other employment and because he's a busy man, Mr. Decker prefers you in residence at his house to be available as-and-when. Is that a problem?"

I have zero desire to relocate to what Sid disparagingly called Decker Island, but I'm also a little intrigued to see how you convert a Victorian prison built on a small islet in The Thames into a home. Anyway needs clearly must. "It's fine."

"Good. Here's Mrs. Canning's card for any practical queries. And the contractual conditions as written are acceptable?"

I'm given time to scan the dense text. The schedule's easily achievable. Most of the rest extends the NDA I signed earlier into a mass of security precautions banning recorders, computers, and outside communication in general. It smacks of paranoia, and that warms me because non-secrets of the no-story kind surely wouldn't merit such fuss.

I especially like the iron prohibition of my ever accessing the first floor of the main house. Why so specific? I sign the document, but - out of professional necessity if nothing else - taking the view that it's my body doing so and therefore only it is constrained by these clauses.

The other part of me retains its right to wander.

7.

I'm packing ready to head east tomorrow when there's a knock at the door. At my flat's door! As in without the street entry buzzer having rung.

I approach the peep-hole cautiously. Despite the absurd cost of this tiny rectangle of West London it has only a fifteen-pounds Yale lock holding a thin pine door shut. One firm kick would open it up.

I bend and squint through. The elderly-but-spry man on the other side is watching for this. "Good afternoon Mr. Harrison. My name's Hughes. Can we have a little chat?" he says quietly near the door in a moderated but still East London accent.

I have this nagging feeling I recognise his thin, hard-lined face. Hughes? Hughes? Then it comes back: Harry 'Hangman' Hughes of the Metropolitan Police force. Elder brother of the murdered Detective Constable Brian Hughes, and so obsessively on the trail of Sid, Danny and all their gang that he delayed retirement to stay on the case. I let him in, because whatever this is surely isn't going to leave unheard.

"Thank you kindly Mr. Harrison. I appreciate your trust."

I direct him to the bed-sofa, which fortunately I've put into sofa form for the day, and take my writing chair.

"Now, am I right in guessing you recognised me at the door?"

"Yes. Detective Chief Inspector, isn't it?"

"For my sins. Emeritus might be a bit more accurate these days. Anyway, a little birdie tells me that you're about to take a working vacation on Decker Island...?"

I try to disguise my shock that he knows this, and I'm fairly sure I fail. "It was a free country last time I checked," I say haughtily.

He holds his hands up. "Oh of course, of course. I've nothing but the highest respect for our country and its laws. A patriot I'd call myself, in fact. How about you Mr. Harrison? Are you a patriot?"

"That's a word that can be twisted, but broadly, yes."

"Nice to hear. And your views on murder, Mr. Harrison?"

"Obviously I in no way condone it."

"Good. Good. So if you happened to be interviewing a known murderer in order to write his autobiography, and if some details about how he killed his victims were to slip out, your instinct would be to let the authorities know, right?"

I don't like where this is going, so - God bless Oxford University and all who sail through her - take refuge in semantics. "What confuses me, Detective Chief Inspector, is that you, representing said authority, seem to be declaring him a murderer in order to push me to obtain the evidence needed to prove him a murderer. Is that not flying in the face of judicial presumption of innocence?"

I don't doubt he dislikes me as a smart-arse, but he keeps it well hid. "If we presumed everyone innocent we'd never mount an investigation and catch a criminal. You're right that I can't force you to tell me anything, Thomas. I'm asking for your help finding my brother's killer. Terry Norris' too of course."

Something occurs to me now, something I remember Sid being very smug about when we did the chapter on his courtroom dramas and got as near as we ever did to talking about these two deaths. "But does it even matter? Sid Marsh and Danny Decker were already tried for those murders and found not guilty. Doesn't double jeopardy prevent them from being re-tried for the same crime?"

Hughes' eyes light up in a way that unsettles me. "It won't when Part 10 of The Criminal Justice Act 2003 becomes law in a week or so. Then I'll have another chance. Then I can finally get those bastards behind bars where they belong."

He realises he's gone overboard and falls back on a good cop routine, all decent-bloke, chummy and confiding. "See between you and me, Thomas, new forensics technology used on the pin from the grenade that killed my brother identifies the DNA we found there as Danny Decker's. Now we've got some legal hurdles with the process not being ratified yet, and with how we got Mr. Decker's sample to make the match, but if you care about truth then the answer's clear. I know he committed those murders. After all you must have seen and heard writing Sid's book for him I'm sure you've no trouble believing it. So all I'm asking for is any little extra you can get me to make the case watertight. The only question, really, is whether you're going to do the decent thing for justice and society should the chance arise?"

I don't reply. I don't know how to reply. Ghostwriters don't swear any form of Hippocratic Oath. A Hypocritic Oath would be more apt: 'I swear to exploit the author's vanity and massage the truth sensationally in the name of flogging books'. But Brian Hughes' life was stolen from him, and the toll of that on his brother is visible. For all that I don't want the responsibility, he has a point about civic duty and it gives validity to asking me this. What's more, I have my special talent for finding secrets out. If I wished to help I surely could. It puts me in a serious quandary.

"Look Thomas, I understand if the risks involved make you nervous. This would be a high profile conviction, so if it came down to it there could be a new life for you. You'd be well set up and everything arranged. Canada or New Zealand if you like. Nice view of mountains over the lake for writing your novels. Think about it, okay? And get in touch any time of night or day with anything, however small."

He rises, hands me a business card, taps his forehead either in salute or to instruct me to consider carefully, and sees himself out.

I slump onto the sofa-bed, which is comfortable as neither but there's not room for both, and try to get my thoughts to line up.

Terry Norris was a slick, over-handsome cockney who had a knack for finding stuff out, hence the nickname 'Nosey'. He came into Sid's orbit while rationing was still in force after World War Two, and their combined talents made both men a lot of money on the black market. Indeed, Sid regaled me with several derring-do tales of nylons and bananas sneaked off ships as they sailed the Thames estuary up to the docks.

But whilst Sid doggedly employed cunning, charm, logistics and threat to build his empire on these profits, Terry's riches would take their leave of him in the next card game or horse race. He felt cheated, grew resentful and envious of Sid, and in some weak moment succumbed to the overtures of the Metropolitan Police Force, as proffered by Detective Constable Brian Hughes.

Following in his brother's law-enforcing boot-prints, the younger Hughes had been training and serving up in Hertfordshire. This would enable him to 'go in clean' undercover in the East End. Or so the police thought. One evening in 1975, Brian, posing as a visiting inspector for one of the high rise developments being built to replace the old slum streets, met Terry for an exchange of money and information. Neither made it out of the parked car they were using for this. The exact details are unclear, because no witness testimony could be secured, but their tête-à-tête was interrupted by a hand grenade pushed in through the part-open window, and the end result looked like so many tomatoes in a blender.

Sid Marsh kept himself at arm's length from said grenade by conveniently dining in a packed restaurant three miles away. Did he order the hit? Did Danny, whose sudden promotion to Sid's side followed almost immediately, carry it out? Most people have always assumed so, but nothing could be proven. In the East End grassing up your own to the coppers is the cardinal sin, and every line of enquiry about the murders was met with a deafening chorus of 'dunno's and 'no idea guv's.

Sid was pressed extensively, but maintained he'd no idea Terry was selling information and had no knowledge of who had killed him and Brian Hughes. He kept to this same line with me while we were doing his book, and the narrative makes an eloquent defence of his innocence. I didn't believe that when I was writing it, and I still don't. He might not have allowed it into words, but I've no doubt Sid hated Terry with hellish ferocity.

Harry Hughes fought to be the detective in charge, but years dragged by without his ever being convinced he had enough to secure a conviction. Frustrated, he targeted Sid's empire and people by foul as well as fair means. Eventually the negative publicity around the obvious vendetta became too much even for The Force, and Harry was relocated to Hampshire and a training and development role behind a desk. His successor had Danny and Sid arraigned in court on a double murder and accessory-to charge inside a month. Three weeks of high-profile trial later, Sid was acquitted and walked free. Danny was also found not guilty of the murders, but was convicted of the lesser charge of perversion of the course of justice and sentenced to six months.

But two corpses and no killers is bad maths that a lot of people still want an answer to. As you know, I was curious enough myself to investigate, even if I couldn't share whatever I found.

Beyond a point I really couldn't get into Sid's head. But whilst appearing to nap on a warm afternoon in his back garden I was able to enter his locked office for a ferret around. With police raids always a possibility he was never going to leave any clear mea culpa written down, but I did discover a receipt in a tax declaration folder. The morning after Norris and Hughes were killed, Sid ordered a gold-plated Smiths Imperial wristwatch to be inscribed on the back with "World's Best Cleaner." My hunch has always been that you'll find this wristwatch on the hand that pulled the pin from that grenade.

I'd half-wondered if Danny Decker might be wearing it when I met him. He wasn't, of course. But if it turns up on his island? If writing his story comes with proof that he murdered two men?

I do not know. I just do not know.

I burn Hughes' card over the sink because I'm getting aware of how easily secrets can be found out. But not before encoding his two phone numbers with tiny dots on the respective characters of consecutive lines on page 112 of a book I'm taking with me for leisure reading.

It's a fairly lightweight novel, as they go, but it's always good to have an escape. Especially if you might end up doing something to provoke a dangerous situation.

8.

I've never even heard of the Docklands Light Railway stops out here. I'm going to be met at the Pier Road exit from King George V station, and spotting the two men isn't hard; I've had Frank Geyser fight off dozens of similar-looking low-level cogs in the East End machine. They direct me into the back of their car and they get in the front. We drive no more than a couple of minutes to an anonymous light industrial building in an area all closed up because it's Sunday. A steel-reinforced garage door rolls up to admit us, and then closes to lock us in.

I follow the men into a back room where a third man, who looks like the first two if they'd specialised in science rather than physical education, runs an airport-style hand-scanner over me. I remove my watch and my belt and he does it again and seems satisfied, moving on to my medium-sized suitcase.

I'm irked by it all, especially when my trusty little red Nokia 8210 is requisitioned and I have to say my pin code out loud for everyone to hear. Tech-acolyte plugs it into a computer and does God-knows-what.

"Can't let you 'old on to this at the property," he says, dropping my phone into a small plastic bag. "If you 'ave to use it ask Mrs. Canning."

I'm tempted to kick up a fuss, but I need this job and I also don't need my phone for much more than playing Snake, which I've been meaning to go cold turkey on anyway. Mother already knows I'll be incommunicado for a few weeks, and the sad fact is that if anyone else even notices my absence they're unlikely to be bothered by it. It occurs to me at this point that I really do keep everyone I know at too much distance.

The goon moves on to unpacking my case and holding up each garment to inspect. He's better than me at folding though, and returns my unremarkable luggage in a neater state than it was. No goodbyes are exchanged, and I follow the first two men out through the back door.

We're on the banks of The Thames now. River mist is building, and it's cold and smells bad. A small launch waits at a tiny jetty, and I'm directed on board. Its stringy, granite-hewn pilot is old and a little bent, but still as tall as my six-foot-three. He nods to me and I almost want to gush gratitude. It's easy to think this whole kind of cold treatment will be water off a duck's back, but it's well-designed to get to you fast. And I'm vulnerable because, whilst I recognise I have no choice about doing this, I just wish I could close my eyes and everything would go away. Really there's nothing much in life I'd miss.

The pilot goes into the little cabin and holds the door for me to follow. It smells of tuna sandwich. I sit on the hard bench seat while he takes the wheel and sets the boat moving downstream. It's flat and grey and industrial on either side of the expanse of river that spawned England's great city. The only tall thing here is electricity pylons, and soon they are lost to the growing fog. Raindrops are spattering on the condensation-smeared windows, and it seems colder inside this dubious shelter than out. The grey thins and there's a glimpse of Crossness pumping station, then it's gone but the smell of the sewage treatment plant stays with us.

Sewage isn't welcome in West London; we make our share of it, but then it's apparently sent east, the direction of the river presumably our convenient excuse. The stink mixes with the odours of sandwich and diesel and the pitching of the boat and I start to feel unwell. I think I can manage not to throw up, but I'm getting a thumping headache.

We chug onwards, still without a word being spoken, and I guess from the turn we've passed Coldharbour. On our left now is Rainham Marshes, and dead ahead, emerging from the gloom, is the tiny island that's our destination.

There was something there anyway; there are Tudor-era references to a fort in the river in this place, but probably nothing more than a timber platform fixed onto a rare firm patch of riverbed. It was the Victorians, in the 1840s, who first hauled thousands of tons of stone here to create the outer form of the island, and then barge after barge of broken brick and quarry rubble to fill it in so it could be built upon. Perhaps its purpose, isolating select prisoners for various reasons of empire, was modelled on the Tower of London. Certainly the architecture is of the same school, although with less ostentation. It's stained and grim and forbidding, with three storey high walls around its whole perimeter, save where a drawbridge - currently raised - can open onto a car-width pier to the north bank of the river, and to the south where there's an area of grass with a tree and the jetty we're heading to.

They named this place Penitent's Isle.

There's no reception party for me. The boatman ties up and drops a plank into place, which I wobble down unsteadily. Being on land feels strange now, and my head's thick as the fog. There's a small shed up against the wall and a gravel path leading on from there past the tree, which I think is an apple even though there's no fruit on it. I notice that there's a track worn through the grass, going from the path to the tree, on to a small promontory which is as far as you can get from the buildings on land, and back to the path. It puts me in mind of animals in a small field or perhaps prisoners in an exercise yard; somehow it shrieks penned-in.

Round a protruding corner of wall there's a door of iron-bound oak set into the stonework. It has a rusty keyhole, but the boatman takes out a remote control, presses a button, and there's a clunk like the unlocking of an upmarket vehicle. He pushes the door open and gestures me through to get my first glimpse of the inside of Penitent's Isle.

To my left is a small, utilitarian cottage built out from the wall. After it, incongruously, is a sizeable allotment with neat rows of vegetables. Beyond that is a larger, single-storey stone building alongside the drawbridge. This, along with a gravel drive finishing at a covered parking area containing three sleek black cars, makes up one half of the heart-shaped interior formed by the grim, turreted walls. The entire other half is the main building to my right. Its stone façade is as austere and forbidding as you'd expect of a prison, but because it's Victorian they couldn't resist decorative touches. Rainspout gargoyles snuck their way into the designs. Columns, of course, around the door and windows. Even a few finials are present to hint at the wealth of empire. Low bushes at either corner make a forlorn effort at softening things, but ultimately this place was always designed to look hard.

Which may explain why it resonates so much with Danny Decker that he chose to live here.

A thin, beady-eyed woman of advancing years emerges from the main house and meets us in the centre of the gravel. She looks as stern as the architecture. "Mr. Harrison, I'm Mrs. Canning, the housekeeper. This is Eric, the groundsman. You'll be in the guest quarters." She indicates the little cottage by the gate we came in through. "Shall we?"

I follow her, Eric loping silently behind us. The hallway opens onto a small lounge, which I see has been set up as a study with a desk, a good chair, pens and several notebooks.

"You should have all you'll need. Eric or I will collect you when Mr. Decker has time for you. For anything else use the phone to the main house. Don't come over or go looking."

"Okay," I acquiesce. "But can I have at least a laptop to work on?"

"That won't be possible. Mr. Decker doesn't hold with them on the island. Use the books to make notes, and you can type things up later after you're done here and when what you're taking away's been vetted and approved."

My handwriting is such an appalling scrawl that I often can't read it myself, but I suppose for the fee that's on offer I can adapt. "A tape recorder?"

The look she throws me is withering. "No. The bedroom and bathroom are through here, and the kitchenette should have all you'll need for breakfast and cups of tea and coffee. Eric will bring your meals over, lunch at one and dinner at six-thirty."

I'm still queasy from the boat ride, and my headache's got worse rather than better. It's a bigger and better space than my flat, but all I can think of is how claustrophobic it feels. "And if I need a spot of fresh air and exercise?"

She frowns. "Will that really be necessary?"

"Well, yes! Look, my job here involves learning and then ordering a whole lot of information. If I just sit staring at the notebooks I'll go mad. If I want to go for a walk round Rainham Marshes is there a way I can lower the drawbridge?"

Both of them bite down on their reactions, but this idea clearly appals them. Do they fear an invasion or something?

"That is not possible," Mrs. Canning asserts, again.

"Then could I at least borrow a key for the gate to go out to the bit of grass where the boat docked?"

Mrs. Canning glances at Eric, whose oaken face bends itself to look equivocal.

"I suppose," she admits grudgingly. "Eric will get you one. Now, as Mr. Decker won't be back until the morning I'll leave you to settle in. Remember, use the phone to the house for anything you need. Don't go wandering."

Pursing her lips and still radiating offence about the key, she bustles out and Eric follows her. I look out the window and see him walk over to the gatehouse. She, meanwhile, crunches across the gravel and goes up the steps and into the main building.

'Wandering'. How ironic that she should choose that word! But there are three reasons for not doing any of that yet.

Firstly, I want to see what I get in person. If nothing else, the contrast between that and what I later learn ex-persona will be revealing.

Secondly, as per Tarquin's meeting with The Witch, knowing relevant secrets can be a heavy burden, and not one I'm good at bearing. I want to appear innocent under the scrutiny of these people's well-honed suspicions, and the best way to achieve this is to genuinely know no secrets for the time being.

And thirdly, I'm certain that I'm coming down with something. That makes wandering a much more difficult exercise, limiting my range and my time away. I don't know why the body wants to keep the spirit close in times of sickness, but the fact of it remains. That essential bond feels somehow strained by ill health.

It raises a spectre: the fear of losing contact. How easy it might be to make a mistake that proves fatal.

9.

I wake up mangled by dreams. It takes me a full minute to work out where I am and why. I wish I wasn't. It feels like there was someone else in the room during the night, but given this place must have gruesome history by the bucketload I suppose I'm just imagining things. My head is discomfited with the onset of a cold, and the foul scents from yesterday's boat trip seem to linger on right through me.

So begins the morning, but as usual the mind grinds into gear and recalls its various reasons for doing all the things it doesn't want to do - money, mortgage, career, etcetera - eventually acquiescing to the map of the coming hours.

Shuddering, I do the deed and cast aside the duvet. Rise, sit back down again so my head stops pounding, and then restart at a more moderate pace. I try to dredge up enthusiasm for my task here, but I'm not succeeding.

I've said it before: doing Sid's book shredded my nerves. Our sessions were like delving into a bran tub filled with mousetraps, because ask a question too many about too sensitive a subject and his gaze would harden and I would KNOW that real people had been really hurt by this man and it wasn't all just salt-of-the-Earth Cockney fun and games. And yet from our first session, where Sid recounted my fraudulent winning of that book prize and let out his infectious guffaw, it was also clear he had stories to share and appreciated my technique for the telling of them. He was a raconteur, and, most importantly, keen to see his life in print. A laundered version anyway.

Today, though, I have to find a way into Danny Decker, and I'm grimly certain it's going to be like getting blood out of an angry stone.

Why that palpable sense of reluctance? If he's not afflicted by the normal vanity of the genre then why on Earth invite the spotlight of publication to shine upon his past and present? Three years ago, when he first made contact, I could understand Sid's unflattering portrayal needling him into a reply. But still?

And then why never hire another ghostwriter? Heaven knows there are enough of us hiding out there in plain sight. Why me?

The phone's harsh bell interrupts.

"Mr. Harrison, Mr. Decker will see you in ten minutes. Eric will come to collect you."

"Please call me Thomas." As ripostes go it's weak, not least because Mrs. Canning has already hung up.

I finish dressing, eat some cereal direct from a packet in the kitchen, burn my tongue on instant coffee - which now tastes unpleasant to me - and am ready with notebook and pencil when Eric's knock rattles the door.

We walk across the gravel drive and I force my biographer eyes and mind to start working. Apart from my subject, is it only Mrs. Canning and Eric who live here? They aren't much older than him, but are they some sort of surrogate mum and dad for a man who had so little parenting he might as well have been an orphan? That could be interesting to explore, but in Danny's case family would be a risky place to start the questions. If I'm going to prise open this East End oyster then pride is a gentler way in, so his house is a better topic. It's clearly had no expense spared, and it's an actual island in the Thames complete with an interesting history. Yes, this is surely how I get Danny Decker talking; his manor, complete with its still-raised drawbridge to the wider world.

We ascend the main house steps and go into a broad, tiled hallway. The third door on the right opens to an airy room that's a nice mix of comfortable study and library. Eric ushers me inside and withdraws. It has windows looking southeast over the river, and with the walls coming right out of the water it feels like we're on some sort of luxury liner. Books on shelves cover all the interior walls. There are stacks and stacks of them, so many they would put an average small-town library to shame. Unlike those in the office of The Topaz Table, these are novels. And, from what I can see, most are nice editions too.

This is a collection of stories for pleasure, and collated with at least a kind of love.

Danny enters from the hall. His emotions are hard to read, but I'd say this morning finds him tired and irritable. "Thomas," he greets me, extending a hand which I shake. "Did you sleep alright? You don't look great."

"Just a touch of head cold or a reaction to the boat trip. I don't seem to be much of a sailor." Sid would have had a bawdy joke in reply, but Danny ignores the aside.

He directs me to where two leather chairs face each other across a coffee table, and we sit. "So where do we start? What's your process?"

"There's no set method. We just talk. As we go I'll sometimes make notes to ensure I have the facts right, but in my head I'll be assembling the pieces into an overall story and also trying to get a feel for your voice. Then we'll focus and fill in towards something complete, and you review periodically to be sure you're happy with the way it's evolving."

"Doesn't it piss you off that your name's never on the books you write?"

Not the question I was expecting. Autobiography subjects typically grab every opportunity to gush about themselves - Tarquin's theory about his vanity publishing clients is that their nearest and dearest are sick to the eye teeth of it and ghostwriters are cheaper than psychiatrists per hour.

"No, not really. I think it lets me be more objective. And to be honest I prefer to stay out of the limelight."

This is at best an expediently-contrived half-truth, and his face leaves little doubt he notices. Being caught in any kind of lie is exactly how I didn't want to start these sessions. I curse my thick head and try to reclaim some initiative.

"So it's an incredible and unique property that you have here. Perhaps we can begin with what made you buy it? It was back in the eighties wasn't it?"

"No. I bought it in '79 to use for storage and the like. 1983 was when I decided to live here and had it renovated."

"Sorry, my mistake. And was it completely derelict when you got it? It must have been a massive project."

He sighs as if discussing this is tedious. "It fell into disuse in the early 1900s, was manned by various garrisons during World War Two, and then got left to rot because the MoD had no use for it. The builders had to gut the place and redo it from not much more than the outer walls."

"That must have been fascinating. I bet you uncovered all sorts of history?"

"Nothing we didn't expect."

"But I suppose you designed the layout yourself, and after twenty years here it must really feel like home now?"

"Are you saying I'm getting on?" He attempts it like a quip, but he's not a quipper.

"Not at all. I know you were born in 1945 but I'd honestly never have guessed it. Would it be interesting to show me round?"

"Listen, I'm not bothered about doing Grand Designs. This place has good privacy and I like being on the river. It was convenient, okay? Next."

Next, I think, I bang my head repeatedly against the wall before going to the nearest lottery ticket vendor for a slim chance of being able to quit this job. "Understood. Well then I suppose the conventional place to start is your early years. The East End took so much damage during the war; it was half in ruins. What was it like growing up there?"

Danny shrugs. "Hard. But then it's always been hard, hasn't it?"

"Would you say it still is? You know, like it used to be? There's been a lot of very ambitious redevelopment."

Finally I elicit an emotional response, but it's a sneer. "The war certainly gave them that chance."

"Gave who what chance?" I grab at this open goal.

"The smug do-gooders in positions of power who always think they know best. They want to 'fix' the East End, but without ever understanding the place or its people. They spout 'duty to society', but what their concept of duty boils down to is us being servants in a setup that has them sitting pretty. They come along with a bundle of taxpayers' cash to pay for their grand projects - not their own money, which they have lawyers and accountants making sure they barely pay tax on. They shove the locals aside so they can play god, and then they're off back to Knightsbridge and Hampshire at the weekends, haw-hawing away to their friends about how they and their charitable consciences have nobly improved the lot of the underclasses. And like as not they'll never again set foot in the place they've turned on its head."

I happen to think he's got a fair point, and it makes me conscious of my relatively-Queen's-English accent. "Leaving a vacuum here that people who do understand the East End can build empires in?" I divert.

He gives me a flash of his dead smile. "True. In West London business, politics, law and high society all overlap. Here a lot less so. But don't make the mistake of thinking that equals easy opportunities. They don't have much here, and getting any more than your meagre share is damn hard." He frowns, suddenly seeming to want to move the conversation on. "By the way, I was thinking about titles," he says. "What do you reckon to 'Rock Hard'?"

I reckon my honest reaction would involve barfing all over his expensive rug. "I'm afraid I think one of the 60s supergroups already used it, and it's not a good idea to repeat titles in the same genre."

"Well check that, and also note down any ideas you have."

How about 'I Don't Want To Talk About It', the cussed part of my brain throws out, unhelpfully. "Certainly. But to return to your childhood, what are your earliest memories?"

He shrugs again. "Shouting. Doors slamming. The noise of a can being kicked up and down the street when we couldn't get a football. Hanging around outside Upton Park on a Saturday and the roar when Billy Dare or John Dick scored. Normal stuff."

"It's interesting that all those are sounds. Do you think your eye injury brought those auditory memories to the front?"

"No. It just meant I couldn't box anymore unless I wanted to go blind."

"And how was it you first got into boxing? You were a real talent from all I've heard."

"Heard from Sid?"

I decide to bite that bullet, because I'm losing the will to live trying to get this guy started. "Yes. He said he felt responsible when you got the injury because he'd organised the bout. He reckoned you could have turned pro and done decently."

"No, or that left hook would never have connected with me. And Sid never did anyone a favour that didn't have payback for him in it somewhere down the line."

"But your boxing career must have stood you in good stead for your later business ventures? As you mentioned, the East End is a hard place, and you had to be able to both deliver and take some blows I bet. Well, 'Rock Hard': you've already said as much."

The same shrug yet again. "You do what you need to, don't you?"

I nod, wishing I had a pillow to scream into.

Seventy-two gruesome minutes that felt like hours later, and thank heavens Danny has to go off to The Topaz Table. He walks me out as far as the gravel, makes a quick call on a handheld walkie-talkie, gets a reply, and then the drawbridge lowers just long enough for him to drive out.

What have I got? He grudgingly confirmed that he never knew who his father was and that his mother died after a long illness when he was seventeen. He was short and thin as a child, which I imagine was from malnourishment. Not that I can put this into the book, because that would be to criticise his dear old mum, bless her wheezing alcohol-sodden soul. She would appear in the street in her dressing gown to search the bins, and Danny was picked on badly as a result but learned to fight back. And I can't use this either because it came from Sid, and I didn't dare go anywhere near it in conversation with Danny. All I have is that boxing was what kids did in the East End because it was a tough place, and he was quick and - bien-sûr - hard, and it was a good way to be the man of the house and bring home some useful money.

The only topic I was remotely able to get him elaborating freely on was his long-running battle against the London Irish, which he characterises as having been for Queen and country, hinting strongly that his intervention prevented a number of planned IRA bombings in the capital. This might be a viable angle with today's Al-Qaeda terrorist threat and so on, but not without the names, dates and other specifics which he flat out refused to give me.

And that's been the day's problem in a nutshell. Any time I push for detail I think he must hear a detective inspector's accent probing for evidence and clam right up. For a genre readership that feasts on specifics it's a non-starter. And where Sid provided rich characters and personal histories for good filler, Danny is a dry well. What makes me a professional writer is my ability to see a book, and I have nothing. Okay, it's the first day, but still.

So is it time to go wandering?

No. All three of my reasons not to do that remain valid. Once the notes I've made are all ordered and written up, I'm going to take two of the ibuprofen Mrs. Canning brought me and to my bed. Tomorrow can only be better than this.

Or tomorrow can be more of the same.

We only did fifty-five minutes today, and I think Danny hates it as much as I do.

There is no rapport, and this process requires rapport. Flattery falls flat. Sycophancy elicits only looks of contempt. The conclusion I keep coming back to is that he's being forced into doing this, but he's clearly the boss of his world so that makes zero sense. I'm at a loss. I also woke up again feeling I'd been watched in the night, and I'm bunged up to the nines so my whole skull hurts.

I detail the drab dialogue diligently, but it's as much about demonstrating fulfilment of contract to ensure payment as it is a nascent book.

I start my third day of incarceration on Penitent's Isle by using the key Eric brought me last night with dinner. It was another haunted and uneasy night, and it's a relief to pass through the little gate and outside the walls to the small patch of grass.

I go to the tree, which is indeed an apple. Then I go to the dock, which is a basic structure of posts sticking out of the brown-grey river. The boat isn't here. Lastly the small shed up against the wall, which appears to be both locked and just for storing boat and gardening junk. To the southeast of the expanse of lapping Thames lurks the brown-and-beige monster that is Littlebrook power station, and just beyond it the giant span of the Dartford Crossing bridge, where the M25 appears tailbacked.

At least my nose seems clearer today, although sense of smell is a dubious benefit in this part of the estuary.

I spot that faint path again and follow it. It takes me out on the tiny promontory, right up to the water's edge. Here, if you lean, it's almost possible to see round the island's southeast tower to its eastern face, and I'm intrigued to spot a sliver of glinting sunlight reflecting from the upper floor. I can't see any more though, and to stretch further would be to risk falling headfirst into the opaque water, so I retreat. Perhaps there will be another yard or so of ground at low tide, affording a better view. It's a tiny little thing to anticipate, but for now I've been out here a while and need to be at the main house's beck and call, so I return to the cottage, shuddering as I re-enter the embrace of the walls.

The phone rings not long after I get back, then Eric's at the door and we traipse across the gravel. It's already a prison-like routine. I go into the study-stroke-library, again wishing I could just enjoy the books instead.

Danny starts our session with a question. "So how's it going, Thomas. Are you getting all you need?"

I'm relieved he's brought this up so I don't have to. "In some ways yes, but in others no. I appreciate that you wouldn't want to implicate yourself in anything the law might consider criminal, and especially cases that remain officially unsolved - Hughes briefly flickers into my mind, but I have enough problems for now so shut that right down. But remember you've got full editing rights over the manuscript to fix anything like that. Danny, to make a story out of this that people will want to read, well you're going to have to give me more. More detail about the most contentious things that have happened in your life and times, and more of the personal side too. The genre demands it."

Danny's face doesn't betray his thoughts, but he takes such a long pause that it's decidedly uncomfortable. "I won't bother asking if you've ever been inside," he says finally. "But have you ever known someone who's been in prison? Visited one?"

"No, I haven't," I admit.

"See no-one from the East End could give that answer. Prison and the courts and the police is how outsiders control the people who live here, and they use those things disproportionately. I mean go back not all that far in history and what would get you a slap on the wrist in the Home Counties would see an East Ender deported to Australia. Think the attitude behind that double standard's changed all that much? As someone who's been put away twice I can correct you on that score. When I got sent down in '79 it was by a bent judge based on fake evidence, so that's why you give them nothing at all. Understand?"

"Yes I do, Danny, but you've contracted me to write your autobiography." My frustration's bubbling towards boiling point. "Giving me nothing simply doesn't work for that."

"I've given you plenty about the Irish."

"That's true, but it's not enough. A publisher will want to print your story because it answers questions the public have. Right or wrong, you're known for your involvement in what the police and the newspapers would term gangland culture and crime. To see your book in print that's where it will have to go. There and into the personal side, even if that's uncomfortable."

Danny considers this. "Know the name Harry Hughes do

you?"

I try to show no reaction, but I'm not certain I manage. Surely he can't have found out, can he? Surely Hughes covered his tracks when he came to my flat? But then Danny somehow discovered I write Frank Geyser, which is the second-biggest secret I possess. "Yes. Detective Chief Inspector in the Met and brother of Brian Hughes." I omit the adjective 'murdered'.

"Right. Well it was old Hangman Hughes who bent that judge and who set up the false testimony that put me back in prison. Okay, it was just on the perverting justice charge and not for murder, but do you think if I could prove what he did there would be any negative consequences for him?"

"Presumably," I offer.

He laughs nastily. "Not a chance. The very worst getting an East Ender wrongly convicted will bring someone like Hughes is temporary suspension on full pay. Because they're all in it together, and even if you show clear as day that there's been a miscarriage of justice they'll believe someone like me deserved what he got anyway. They have us pegged as criminals before we even set foot in court. True justice in London is an illusion. We know that round here, and that's why we don't talk. Not to the cops and not to the papers."

This is like listening to a stuck record. "I understand that Danny. But the issue remains that you're asking me to write your autobiography..." This has to be risked. If I don't it's impossible. "Look. Fall back on 'no comment' at times if you wish, but none of this is being recorded in any way apart from in this notebook, which you've got full control over. You need to make this a safe space and trust me enough to let me ask any and all questions in it. To give me at least most of your answers. If we can't do that then it makes it near-impossible to work together." I try not to think about the money and how badly I need it. "Remember, the NDA I signed prohibits me from saying anything to anyone about what I hear here."

"Do you think the likes of Hughes would care about that? Or some wigged wonder who wants to put me under lock and key would deem anything inadmissible?"

It feels like even the room itself has perked up with the sudden tension and is watching intently.

"Secrets are secrets, Thomas, even if you've signed some bit of paper promising not to tell them."

Again the look he's giving me makes me wonder if he knows about Hughes' visit...but if so why even let me set foot on this island? "I assume you've read Sid's book?" I'm startled to find anger has seized control of my vocal chords.

He nods resentfully.

"Then reference it against your stash of secrets and you know some things he and I talked about. You also know Hughes hates Sid at least as much as he hates you and would go after him as readily as you. Has that happened in the three years since I worked with him?"

"Sid's in Spain. They'd have to extradite him."

"Danny you have to choose. Either you trust me and I can at least ask you about the infamous and the personal..."

"Or?"

"Or you have the wrong ghost and it would be better to end this here and now." My heart should be racing at the several big risks I'm taking, but it's not. Instead I'm strangely focused.

"You think?"

"Yes."

He eyes me, I believe with an element of newfound respect. "Okay then. Ask what you want."

I may as well go for the big prize. I don't even pause to blink. "In 1975 Terry Norris and Detective Constable Brian Hughes were blown up by a hand grenade thrown into the car they were meeting in. Sid had the motive, but he also had a cast-iron alibi. Harry Hughes thinks you were the one who threw the grenade, and I suspect a majority of the general public do too, even if there wasn't enough evidence for a conviction. What response would you…"

"I did not kill Norris and Hughes," he rasps.

I wish I could throw the DNA evidence Hughes found on the grenade pin in his face. Even so he must see my scepticism.

"Listen. I did not murder those two men. I give you my word on that, Thomas. And for this process to work you also need to trust me, right?"

"True," I acknowledge, even though in ghostwritten autobiography it's not necessarily the case. So do I trust him? I can hold off on deciding that for a few more hours. Tonight is the time to start wandering. As with Sid I hardly expect to find documentary evidence, but how about that 'World's Best Cleaner' watch? If it's here on this island then the man's a liar.

"I'm sorry Danny," I say to backtrack away from the tension. "I've had this head cold since I got here and I've not found my feet in this whole situation yet. That was clumsy of me and I apologise…"

"You already did. Don't apologise too much Thomas, or people will think you're hiding something. That's why I never say sorry, even if I'm dead wrong."

"Really?" And yet I think he just did, a little anyway. "Never?"

"Never. It's good we cleared this up though. If we have to do this autobiography it should be done right."

'Have to do'? That's what I thought. I wish there was a way to ask who's making him and how. "Absolutely. I'm glad we're on the same page too. With that in mind, how about we go back over the incidents with the Irish you told me about yesterday and fill in some of the blanks? Since 9/11 terrorism is in the public conscience, and it seems clear you've helped thwart some attacks right here in the capital. I'm sure readers will want to know more about that."

It's flannel and I'm certain he realises it, but either way we go from there into a productive two hours that give me both a clear chapter and also the impression that, murderer or not, and cynic as he might be, Danny has a surprisingly strong sense of patriotism.

So was Hughes' appeal based on that same virtue valid? I think it's time to go roaming for a hard-evidence answer. It's clear nothing will be just given to me; any awkwardness about illicit secrets will be lost in the sea of awkwardness that's here anyway; and that argument with Danny that should have terrified me has actually given me some vitality back.

Thus when I return across the gravel to my cottage I yawn conspicuously, hoping to forestall any questions anyone might have about the deep, unresponsive and hopefully illuminating sleep I'll soon be falling into.

10.

In the end I wait until well after midnight to depart my body. No-one can see me, but I prefer to steer clear of people and their eyes anyway.

Normally I can make my exit rapidly and at will, but with the cold still in my head my body sniffs and shifts and seems reluctant to let me leave.

When, at last, I manage, the illness remains in my body so my mind's suddenly wonderfully clear as I drift outside and soundlessly across the gravel. Despite the darkness I can see every detail. I've always wondered if I am actually seeing in the conventional way, and I can only assume no. I think it's like feeling the words written on pieces of paper; something perceived more out of the habit of attunement than anything else.

First I visit the gatehouse. I want this to be systematic. Like my cottage, it's in good order but essentially Spartan. Eric snores thunderously in a narrow bed inside a small bedroom. There's a little window onto the vegetable patch and a dresser with old photos in black and white. A short man holds the hand of a tall woman with Eric's same features. They're in Pearly King and Queen getup and nervous about the camera. A terraced house, dirt basic and scrubbed spotless. Eric in his youth in shorts and boxing gloves striking a pose in a forgotten gym somewhere. Angular and rangy, he looks tough as old boots; everything apart from his eyes, which, to me, convey trapped. If he ever married there's no record of it here. I'd date every picture to the 1960s or earlier, and after that it seems he prefers to remember nothing about what he's done in life. I start to feel too much the intruder, so I move on.

There's a workshop, a kitchen and a small lounge with a single chair and reading lamp. At a writing desk there's a pencil but no paper. The only other room in the gatehouse contains electric mains and fuses, a phone, and also a numerical keypad that I assume - because below it the word 'RAISED' glows red - controls the drawbridge. I wonder why, inside such secure outer walls, a door with a heavy-duty three-point bolting system is required? And why is that kept locked? Is this for my benefit? Do they fear that I'll try to escape Penitent's Isle?

This raises the question of whether I am free to leave? It hadn't occurred to me that I might not be, but now a little chill seeps into my bodiless soul. I force my mind away from the subject and onto my reconnaissance of the main house.

Rather than go up the steps to the main door I drift straight through the stone below ground floor level to start in the cellar I'm assuming is there. It's a mistake. It's no more than a low concrete void that's completely empty, presumably because of the risk of flooding, but passing through the dense material to get into it has sapped my strength. I was already below par, and now I won't manage to cover the entire building tonight.

The main house has its forbidding western façade inside the walls, overlooking the gravel drive. Its other three sides are the island's outer walls, which rise sheer from The Thames like soot-stained cliffs. In the centre of the house is a small, flag-stoned courtyard with a single, heavy door into it, and this is where I pass upwards from the cellar. The tiny segment of sky above the looming walls makes even a ghost feel trapped. It's a space designed to destroy resolve. I shudder and exit it hastily. What in God's name possessed Danny to try and make a home out of this place?

The north side of the ground floor contains a kitchen, pantry, store rooms, bathroom and laundry. Beyond those, against the east wall, is what appears to be a suite of rooms for Mrs. Canning's use. Her bedroom is pink upon pink, with everything frilled and a magpie-hoard of trinkets and jewellery populating an oversized dresser. She lies birdlike and still as a corpse in the centre of a vast bed. Off the bedroom there's a chintzy sitting room with a picture window towards the Dartford Crossing. And beyond that, a little unexpectedly, an office. At an oak captain's desk sits an expensive computer, which peeves me because it feels like double standards. Also a set of shelves which are well-stocked with what turn out to be criminal law journals. Beside them on the wall is an Utter Barrister certificate in her name. I don't comprehend how this dovetails with the position of housekeeper and the fact I'm sure she cooks the excellent meals I've been eating, but I resolve to maintain more caution around Mrs. Canning from hereon.

The sadness is gnawing at the edges of my vision now, and I know I'm tiring. The rest of the ground floor, the south-facing side, contains a large lounge and formal dining room, which are as impressive as they appear unused. Lastly the study I've been meeting Danny in. I can only take time for the briefest immersion in his library of books. Most of them are more than merely nice editions; they are first or early ones, some dating right back to the 1800s. And whether under Danny's ownership or before, all show signs of having been well-read.

The overall shape of the three river sides of the house makes half an octagon, and four columnar towers mark its north, northeast, southeast and south corners. I'm over by the last of these when I sense space behind the final bookshelf. Some clever mechanism must open a secret door. I pass straight through to find a tight spiral staircase. It's an exciting discovery. I follow it up one storey to where it ends in a door into a bedroom.

Only the made-up bed and the towels and toothbrush in the ensuite bathroom indicate it's in use, and only Danny's clothes filling the walk-in-wardrobe tell me it's his. The man himself isn't here at the moment. Presumably he's off in The Topaz Table running the Decker empire. His lair is fastidiously organised and utterly impersonal. It apparently contains what he needs to conduct his life and nothing more. The only thing you could call interesting is a slim automatic pistol alongside something like fifty thousand pounds in cash in a fingerprint-locked safe behind a Beaches of Dunkirk painting next to his bed. More hardness. More shell. Maybe that's all there is?

The hallway inwards from Danny's room is wider than my whole apartment. It continues off in both directions. Apart from a series of doors it contains only an ornate grandfather clock - that ticks menacingly and feels almost as if it's watching me - and the grandiose staircase down to the ground floor that I see on my way in each morning. I follow the corridor west, towards the house's front.

The next room is a gym. In the centre hangs a punchbag,

and at its edges a rowing machine, a treadmill and several weights benches. At the back pine-clad doors lead to a changing room and sauna. Gyms hold little interest for me at the best of times, so I return to the corridor and continue onwards, north and then northeast, circling round that oppressive central courtyard. There are four generous, unused bedrooms and bathrooms, after which I've almost come full circle and I can see the clock and Danny's bedroom again. There's only one room left to explore, the east-facing one that the other exit from his bedroom must lead into.

For all that it looks superficially like the other doors, inside the fine carpentry of this one there's steel plate and a high-grade lock. I have to enter through the brickwork instead, because metal is the hardest material of all and the sand-timer of my soul's sadness is running very low. I don't have long left. I'm in his office though, and it's been designed to keep intruders out. Paydirt at last, surely.

There is decoration here, but it's all war paintings and East End boxing photos like the one in Eric's room. I scan them but don't recognise a single face. Two aerial photos in 1970s colour show an unrestored Penitent's Isle. The walls are crumbling and there are trees growing out of the main building roof. He must have spent a fortune fixing it all. Interestingly the pier from Rainham Marshes runs all the way in; chopping away part of it and putting in the drawbridge must have been Danny's modification.

There's a cupboard containing a rack with three rifles and three pistols along with a good stock of ammunition. Alongside it is a set of filing drawers. I'm on borrowed time so I can only make a brief scan of the papers inside it, but Danny's organisation is meticulous and aids my search. The share certificates show Danny's sizeable wealth and how many pies he has his fingers in.

Then I find the folio of photos at the back. They have accompanying notes detailing names, dates, locations, amounts, deeds and drugs. This is far more explosive than the gun cabinet! I recognise the features of politicians, business titans and celebrities. The faces of the undressed young women and men pictured with them in various contortions and degrees of compromise aren't famous, but their profession is obvious enough. As is the reason for this photography undoubtedly being clandestine. I shudder at what an ex-Tory minister who's known for sermonising about morality is doing to the youth bent over before him, and move on.

The brazier and packet of firelighters in the corner is a detail I wish I could include in the book. I wonder how much of all this Danny could burn before Hughes and his bluebottles swarmed through the place? Everything of relevance, I assume; this will have been calculated.

But by way of timepieces there's only a Mondaine clock up on the wall to complement the Breguet watch I spotted in Danny's bedroom. The 'World's Best Cleaner' smoking gun I was hoping for is not to be found, even though I go through all the drawers of the desk in search of it. There is only stationery alongside coded ledgers and another hundred thousand or so worth of crisp fifty-pound notes.

The single anomaly I find is a manilla envelope at the back of the bottom drawer. It contains two things: a stamped but nameless birth certificate signed and dated the 15th of March 1976, and a set of photos all of the same man. They run right the way from childhood through to early middle age, slick good looks curdling as the world fails to deliver for Terry Norris.

I'm getting dangerously weak now. Everything around me has turned grey and repellent and the temptation to dissolve out of it grows large. Even though I should be able to last longer than this, I know I've left returning far too late. I push agonisingly through the wall. The short distance downstairs, outside and back to my tossing and turning form in the cottage is like an eternal tunnel.

I re-enter myself and jerk instantly awake, gasping for breath. I'm freezing and shuddering. I turn on the bedside lamp and see the blankets long-since kicked off to lie on the floor. I barely have the strength to retrieve them and curl up like a foetus.

As my mind regains itself I send soothing thoughts to my traumatised body, promising it I won't leave again until it has recovered properly. As the disharmony ebbs, I feel warmer and know sleep is coming to take me.

Before it does there's just enough time for a realisation: the main house has a second floor, but at no point in my exploration of its entire first floor did I see stairs going up.

11.

He's a ghost! That tall, cautious writer, so capital-E Educated like the tutors Danny used to hire, is a ghost!

And he's a spy.

He's not very visible; he must be background by nature. I'm easier to spot; sometimes I even reflect slightly. I barely had time to hide in the clock when I saw him coming. Those lead weights in the mechanism are a right menace.

I followed him. He did a lap of the first floor, poked around in Danny's office for a bit, then went rushing off back to his body. Is that as long as he can spend out of it? Feeble.

I kept my distance and waited, then drifted in to the same place I've been watching him from these last two nights. He was curled up like a baby, turned pale by just that little excursion.

Perhaps I'm being harsh; he has been ill. Only with a sniffle, mind.

So here's a sudden other member of my species when I'd assumed I must be the only one. Well she was too, of course. But we never met as ghosts because despite Danny's best efforts she never even made it to my age. This one's older than me by several years. He can't have long left.

After about half an hour his face finally relaxes. Because he left the lamp on tonight I can see who he really is. I move in close to study him.

Jesus but he's only background by nurture! How do the English middle classes breed them so bloody meek? He's sharp-minded and he's handsome and that lanky frame of his could be forceful as a hell-hound if he let it uncurl and away from the world of desks and rules. If he'd been born in the East End he'd have been a modern-day pirate king; one of the barrow-boys who learns the game, gets as accepted as you ever can, and then reaches back inside his upbringing for the strength to beat them all.

Instead he's penning Danny's autobiography. What an obscene waste of talent. My doing in part, but I'm surprised Danny's picked it up again given I told him I was over all that. It wasn't like he was ever keen. I guess Mrs. Canning's kept advocating for it, the cautious old fusspot. I thought the gains she was eyeing were marginal at best, but is Danny that worried about the change in the law and Hughes? He brushed it off last time it was discussed, but his actions are telling a different story.

That puts fear into me.

She went when he was inside.

I try to shake myself free of those storm clouds. Seeking distraction, I go over to the desk to grade this writer's writing. There's just enough light to make out the words. It's assiduous notes on Danny versus the Irish. Yawn, yawn, Begorrah and yawn. I can tell from his lettering that not a bit of his heart was in this. His hand is the sort that would scrawl so fast as to become illegible in trying to keep up with his mind, if it were but engaged.

I wish there was a way to read the pages below, but they're surely all like this. He'd keep anything interesting hid. Wisely so, because Mrs. Canning will have been in here snooping whilst the writer is with Danny, and her gimlet eye misses nothing.

I'll need to stand watch too. This one's abilities make any treachery doubly dangerous.

I drift back over to him and I can't resist it; he's of my kind. I reach out and brush his temple with my forefinger. A jolt of electricity hits me so hard that I almost come apart.

No! I will not allow that. And least of all will I allow it now, when it feels like a window in my prison wall has opened.

He stirs uneasily, moans and turns onto his side.

I retreat, for the time being.

12.

I awake from a dream of unparalleled vividness: a young woman standing above me. She's lithe and symmetrical with curling brown hair framing a creamy, lightly-freckled face. Her grey eyes are lit with crackling intelligence and...ferocity. It's not quite the right word... Words have never failed me before. But she COMPREHENDS. Comprehends me, what I am. All of it! It's completely disorientating. She's so beautiful to me that it makes my every fibre ache. She reaches her hand towards me, then there's a lightning bolt.

The vision won't leave and I'm at-sea and clumsy as I get up and dressed. Epiphany; it's the only noun for this, even though several disquieting adjectives could qualify it for the rational light of day. It's a sense of connection as I've never encountered in my life, nor even realised could exist.

I know I keep my remove from the world and do most things by halves. I've been largely not-uncontent with that. Yes, perhaps the grass is greener, but the pasture around me has always contained reasonable-enough fodder.

No longer though. Now I Ache and I Yearn and it Hurts to have Lost what I've glimpsed. Passion has suddenly infected my blood! Exclamation marks. Uppercase. All because of a snippet of dream? Something I know to be mere delusion because what other possibility is there?

Unless this is how and why I begin to die.

I can make no sense...

Nor do I have more time to try, because the phone rings and Mrs. Canning is ordering my presence. Today she's given me fifteen minutes notice. That's five minutes more than the previous days, but right now I feel I'd need a lifetime to get into any kind of fit state.

"...but I don't want it to come over as soft."

Danny is, at least, seeing a book. A deadly dull one though. Even so, it's a start for a ghost to pick apart and improve. But I keep tuning out and back to my dream, and I know I'm failing to do the needed here.

"Danny, tell me about Bella."

I cannot believe I've asked that out loud. You could hear a pin drop.

Bella Decker-nee-Marsh, Sid's daughter and Danny's wife. Of whom I saw not a single picture during last night's reconnaissance. Why not? Is it too painful for him? Sid certainly had photos of her. They were everywhere in his 'gaff', constant reminders of his lost daughter's luminous and otherworldly beauty.

A beauty exactly like the woman of my dream.

How did I not realise this before?!

Was I visited by Bella's ghost?

When Danny finally growls "What do you mean?" I can only gawp stupidly at him. He would flare into violence if he knew I had thoughts like I'm having about the love of his life. And for all I'm a head taller, we both know he could kill me.

"Thomas? Hello? What do you mean, I said. How is my wife relevant to what we're writing?"

"Because no man is an island."

"What are you talking about? Are you losing the plot here?"

He looks dangerous, and he's right, I am. I try to make myself climb back in from the ledge. "I'm sorry Danny. Like I said, I caught some sort of nasty cold on the boat ride here. My head's been a bit out of it ever since, and I've been feeling especially rough all this morning. Sorry."

It's lame, and as he assesses me I'm expecting castigation.

"Rough's not really the word that comes to mind when I look at you, you know."

Was that an actual bit of humour?! I smile gratefully. "How about Pillow Hard for the title of my autobiography if I ever write it?"

"Nah. That'd be doing you an injustice. You've just got into the habit of apologising somehow. Twice there a moment ago in fact, which is two times too many."

"One maybe, but I wanted to explain..."

"No. It makes you look weak. It makes you weak."

"What, any admission of fault or failure? Ever?"

"Yes."

"That," I say with sudden feeling, "is a mighty hard road you've set yourself Danny."

His stare doesn't change - he seems only to stare, never just look - but he does blink twice.

"I've never thought about it like that."

He lapses into silence, and I leave it hanging there. At first I'm only glad to have defused the awkwardness, but then I realise the screw is turning on him. I let it. Even the walls seem somehow to be watching closely.

"The second I laid eyes on Bella Marsh my world flipped on its 'ed."

I resist the urge to write this down. Any tiny movement might stop him.

"Sid kept her well away from all his boys of course. Apple of his eye she was, and far better than the likes of us should ever get hopeful about. I'd found an easy groove by then. 'Ad my string of places to collect the money from. I'd sorted the couple of bad apples early so the rest paid up nice and smooth, and I saw to it that they got their money's worth and never 'ad problems. I'd my nice big flat. Any time I wanted to eat out there were a dozen places where'd they'd move a paying customer to give me a good table. Birds too, the real lookers from the clubs. I 'ad it all. Then I locked eyes with Bella, and suddenly it was as if everything I 'ad was nothing at all."

And just like that Danny Decker describes exactly what I'm feeling, except more eloquently than I could have managed. I remain silent and frozen. I'm barely breathing in case I break the spell.

"She was forbidden territory though. Cross Sid on that score and you'd wind up in the river wearin' a pair of concrete boots. We all knew that." He spreads his arms out in a gesture of helplessness. "So there was nothing I could ever do about it."

"But you married her," I blurt out, confused.

"Only after..." And then the shutters slam back down. "Look, I've got a lot to do today, okay? And it's better you go have a lie down and get yourself well. Let me think over whether that whole protection side can go into the book. Of the few places that are left I doubt any would talk, so maybe. We'll pick this up again tomorrow."

It's a dismissal. I rise diffidently, and barely stop myself from trying to walk through the nearest wall rather than detour to the door.

What the hell is up with me today?!

She was just a dream, damn it. An illusion. A spectre.

I don't believe in ghosts.

I, of all people, should know.

13.

I'm gobsmacked that he asked Danny straight out like that. Bella Marsh.

No-one says that name here.

But then Danny only went and answered his question. At least until he caught up with himself and went shtum. Then got angry. Of course. That's his habitual response to stress. And whilst it might serve you well as a boxer or an enforcer or a collector, it's the worst tool for dissecting the complexities of love and loss. He should read more of the novels in his library. He was in such a hurry to get away after that that he nearly let the drawbridge routine slip and I almost had a chance to escape. Mrs Canning was napping, which she never used to do. They're all ageing here on Penitent's Isle though. We're all growing old.

But it's as well he remembered. For all that I sometimes rail against my captor I also recognise that he keeps me safe from myself. It's been going downhill again lately, and I wouldn't trust me at the moment either. No, Danny keeps me near what I need to be near, doesn't he? And it fair kills him to do it. So I suppose I should be grateful.

Thomas went out onto the outside grass afterwards and

tramped around like a tourist. I think he's trying to see the southeast face of the house. I can't imagine why. And if he goes any further he'll step right into the mud.

A filthy power station and a roaring great bridge that never sleeps. That and the jaundiced water is all there is to gaze at from my balcony. Some nights I dream of white sand bordering an azure sea. Tall, jagged cliffs rearing to windswept pines and green hills. Pure air. Three dimensionality.

But that's never going to happen, is it.

The wanderlust is building again, and trying to trick my sanity out of its kennel.

Should I finally let it take me?

Is where it leads a better place?

In the bad times, like these last...well, we're into years rather than just months this time, aren't we? In these bad times only the combined efforts of Danny, Mrs. Canning and Eric stop me from finding out. And the abandon is building even as my guardians wither and weaken.

Except now there's Thomas.

Thomas my fellow ghost.

And I have the strongest feeling that Thomas might change everything.

I resent that, obviously.

But it also excites me.

14.

It's Friday, and my first week on Penitent's Isle ends on an improved trajectory. That mention of Bella broke the ice with Danny, and it's no longer a case of my tiptoeing around a closed book. Not so completely anyway.

True to his word, we cover the protection racket that underpinned both Danny's and Sid's enterprises, for want of a better word. Sid wouldn't elaborate much about all this, but Danny has long since diversified away from it to the extent it's now non-prosecutable history.

And it's a history he's proud of.

At the heart of it is understanding the police as an occupying force little interested in sheltering East Enders from crimes perpetrated by their own. The law is there to contain the East End, protect the surrounding areas of London from its spread, and to uphold the various vested interests the British establishment has here. It's empire in microcosm, and this attitude permeates right down to the recruitment of officers. To be suitable to don the breast-shaped black helmet, a candidate requires the presumption of guilt against all spawned in the East.

I push back at Danny about this, but he's able to reel off a list of blatant miscarriages of justice to support his stance. I take details and will do some independent verification, but I'm already uncertain enough to go with him.

And if you accept this start point then every shop, pub, restaurant and nightclub paying a percentage of their takings for what's effectively a private security service in a lawless realm makes sense. The details he gives me in fact speak of a well-organised business whose fees aren't unreasonable.

"But what about those who prefer to opt out?" I challenge him. "Are they left alone, or is pressure put on them to sign up?"

"How do the police treat people who don't pay their taxes?" is his snapped reply, after which I change the subject.

Not for the first time this week, he seems to fish for details about Sid's personal life. I don't know if it's to test my loyalty or if he hopes to find out what I know about something he's interested in, but either way no good can come of my playing ball, so I dissemble. That leads on to us talking more about his childhood. It sounds so bleak. He was an only child, and burdened with far too much responsibility from far too young an age. Should the parents be blamed for that? Perhaps his dad, except I'm not even sure whoever he was knew he'd fathered Danny.

As for his mother, she was thirteen when the Luftwaffe dropped a bomb on her family's terraced house one night in 1940. She did permanent damage to the tendons in both her hands trying to shift broken brickwork in time to save her buried parents and three younger brothers. She didn't manage. Not any of them.

When society moved on in the fifties and its sympathy for the less notable victims of war waned, she and her bastard son became something for street kids to poke fun at. Danny fought back, bled, filched and begged for food, took paid errands, learnt to cook aged nine, and did his best to look after the both of them.

I don't protest "But you shouldn't have had to because you were just a child," but he reads the thought in me anyway. "There was no-one else," he states factually. It redefines that word 'hard' in my head. Now it's not glamourised gangster bravado, it's the lack of entitlement to a gentler life. It's genuine hardship. And it was and arguably still is right here in this whole compass-point of Britain's filthy-rich capital city, and that makes me ashamed.

Danny added one to his fifteen years to fight in his first backstreet boxing match. He triumphed, and earned twenty-five shillings. He won his second fight too. During the fourth round of his third he was knocked unconscious, and came to dumped in a back alley with his clothes in a pile on the urine-scented cobbles next to him.

I sit through this striving to keep all emotion at arm's length and off my face. It's the requirement of my trade. Emotion must be preserved fresh for the reader to soak in. I am merely the conduit. The ghost in the machine.

Except now staying detached, which was ever my speciality, feels hard.

It was that dream. Bella's ghost.

Some genie has been uncorked inside my head.

I've written everything up, and it's half an hour since I heard the drawbridge fall and then rise again. Danny will spend the weekend at The Topaz Table taking care of business. My week, on the other hand, has ended and I can return to Notting Hill until Monday.

I leave everything neat and arranged on the desk and go outside, where thick grey clouds are producing a light drizzle that hangs in the air. I let myself out through the gate and walk the stretch of grass. The path seems a little less defined. As though someone has ceased walking it lately.

I make my way out to that spit of land and see that it's longer than usual. I must have happened upon low tide. What underlies The Thames isn't pretty, but it looks gravelly and solid enough to risk the extra step. I'm finally able to see round the southern tower, and what was reflecting is a wide, modern glass-railed balcony. I can only see the door onto it side-on, but a light is shining out from inside a room.

A room on a floor to which there were no stairs.

I won't venture there yet, because my body is still traumatised by Wednesday's close call. But there is a secret here on Penitent's Isle, and that secret is up on that second floor.

It's my next trip.

It's also the first time in twenty-one years I've felt afraid at the prospect of wandering.

I notice my foot starting to sink, and I scurry backwards and go to wipe my shoe clean in the damp grass.

At four o'clock prompt I'm waiting out at the dock as Eric arrives with the boat. I don't understand why they can't just let me out via the drawbridge. The afternoon has cleared up and I'd be glad of the mile-and-a-bit walk along the shore path to Purfleet, where I can catch a train.

But no, Mrs. Canning is having none of that, and so I'm once again faced with the sway and stink of a river trip.

Eric keeps the boat steady as I board. This time I make to stand outside the cabin and by the forward railing, hoping it will quell the nausea.

"Can't let you do that," mutters Eric, holding the door open for me.

I don't protest, just go into the little space with its foggy windows. Five days on Penitent's Isle and I'm already institutionalised.

"Here." He hands me the plastic bag with my phone in. "Don't turn it on 'til you're on the tube."

We set off, and it's only when I see Eric glance apprehensively at the now-visible north bank of The Thames that I think to analyse the situation a bit more. Bending to a clearer bit of glass, I see two men standing by a white car. They are watching us openly. One holds a camera with a hefty zoom lens. They aren't wearing uniforms, but there's something about the stance and set of their bodies that's equally identifying.

"Coppers?" I ask Eric.

There's only wide river ahead of our slow boat, but he keeps his eyes fixed on it.

"Yeah," he confirms.

15.

Oh Danny, Danny, Danny. Never call him Danny boy, because that'll set him right off. But how agonisingly childish you've been.

Why does it take an interloper for you to speak of all this? If ghosts could weep I would have soaked every page of every book in the stair door bookshelf.

I've been horrible to you so often, haven't I? But why didn't you show me this side before? Why was it exclusively my demons, my hauntings that we argued about? Am I really so washed about upon the waves of my own troublesome ocean that you denied yourself everything to try and be my anchor?

Or is it just habit? East End pig-headedness and that infuriating refusal to ever admit to getting it wrong.

One way or another you've built walls around you as high and grim as Penitent's Isle's. But Thomas the storyteller somehow has a gate key, and so I've finally glimpsed inside.

Danny went off at a rate, all puffy-faced and uncontrolled. I wonder if Hughes' two rozzers in their car got themselves a nice photo? Even if they did the old git will just assume it's because his chance for revenge draws nearer. The Lords and politicians finished with their flapping protests and settled back down on their velvet perches like the overfed chickens they are, and the new law is due for royal assent on the 20th.

Don't get taken away from me Danny, for only now do I see how much I need you.

I want to say your most hated words to you: I'm sorry.

Don't leave. Please.

Like the solid-bodied can, so sudden and so sure.

Like Thomas vanished just a few hours later.

Will we all reconvene on Monday?

Or will I come apart before then? Will I answer the siren

call at last? It grows stronger, for all that new doubt flickers, and I fear even the defences of Penitent's Isle aren't enough to hold it at bay much longer.

16.

We head west and this time the smell gets less not more. Pylons and cranes and shipping crate mountains give way to architecture. I'm heading back to the genteel part of town. Now I see the imbalance, though. One end of the seesaw stays up only if the other is held down.

Why did I want to live here so badly? I suppose it was because everyone said it was at the heart of things, so where else could a professional observer of life wish to be? But for all that this heart rat-races, the artery-clogged old beast is unloving. It's raucous and filthy, despite its pretences and the many wastes it pushes off to its East. It's old and it's entitled and it's been a vicious swine and an unrepentant thief over the centuries. The wealth of empires built this place, but all riches are as much taken as made, and today it strikes me that I could drain a thousand lifetimes of blood into old London town and it wouldn't offer a single word of thanks.

So much for the heart of things. Ultimately that's just a muscle. What about the soul? Until that vision of two days ago I'm not sure I could have laid claim to having much of one. Now it's out though, and squirting ink over my worldview like an octopus in flight.

We dock. I nod farewell to Eric. There's a gate and an alley and some streets and some trains. I get back to my flat and half expect Hughes to be sitting inside waiting like the warder of it all.

Bella, if that's who you were; what the hell did you do to me? Why did you do it to me? Is there any way back?

I don't want this new awareness of everything.

Being the sleepwalking Thomas was so much easier.

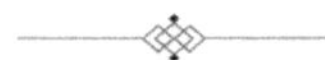

Ten-something and the buzzer rings. "Morning! Royal Mail. Registered delivery packet for Mr. Harrison." I let her up and she hands me a parcel sent by a paper supplies company that I didn't order anything from. I'm about to say it's a mistake, but my name is on it so the postwoman's not at fault and instead I just sign. She hands me two letters as well, one a flyer inviting me to find God, the other a plain envelope, which I open first.

Your flat's bugged. Turn your phone off then go for a long walk and find a café. If it's safe to make contact I'll meet you there.

That clears up the packet mystery then. Hughes, and done cleverly. I consider ignoring the summons, but I still have no idea what I'm going to do or why. Two things tip the balance. The first is vexation at Danny for having his people break in and bug my flat. The second is remembering Hughes' mention of Canada or New Zealand. That kind of restart in a clean space somewhere - a fresh page - feels a remarkably tempting prospect today.

I arrive at Mork & Stark. Elin gives me a quizzical look that morphs into a welcoming smile - possibly faked - and says "Hey". I get the last available nook; they seem busier today, but I suppose it is Saturday.

Hughes slides in opposite me a few moments later.

"Don't ever become a spy Thomas. Jesus wept."

I'm really not in the mood for additional criticism today. "I thought you wanted me to be one?"

"Don't keep looking over your shoulder like that. Try to act natural."

"Are you paying for this?" I've spotted Elin approaching and a tiny revenge for what he's putting me through.

"Of course. We're not cheapskates Thomas. And that would also apply to that new life abroad I mentioned last time. We'd set you up very nicely."

"Hey!"

"Hi Elin. The Panamanian Geisha Arabica for me please. How about you, er, uncle? I recommend it."

"Nah, none of that fancy stuff for me. Just something strong and black."

"The Ethiopian co-operative then," I chip in quickly. No afternoon nap for Hughes today.

Elin, looking genuinely pleased that I remembered, scribbles and leaves and Hughes shakes his head. "I remember when coffee was just coffee."

"But only progress gets rid of the double jeopardy law, right?"

He cocks an eyebrow. "Alright, we'll get down to business then. Had an interesting week have you?"

"So-so. I've found myself re-evaluating a few things."

"Would you care to expand on that?"

"Not really. So I know you're hoping I'll learn some great secret, but they're as careful with me as they are with anyone else. It's not likely."

"They?"

"Look, one thing is if I learn clear evidence about a serious crime, but I'm not going to turn informer for your every question, okay?"

Hughes purses his lips. "Danny been justifying his good heart and patriotism and all that has he?" he asks sarcastically.

"I'm working on his autobiography. Obviously he's been telling me his version of some things."

"I bet he has. Thomas, at any point have you wondered why Danny wants to write this now? He wants what Sid got. Your...can we say selective morals and your gift with words to construct himself a pre-emptive defence. He's guessed for the last few years there's a retrial coming, and he also knows the power of the court of public opinion. I was hoping for at least a courtesy check-in from you, but I guess you've been too busy."

"In fact they took my phone," I say coldly, not liking being called morally selective.

"And if they hadn't would you have called?" Bad cop is near the surface. Hughes is showing his stress. An old man with one last shot.

"As I said, to date I've seen or heard nothing that would help you with what you want. If I did, I don't yet know how I would react."

Hughes considers me. "At least that's an honest answer, which I appreciate. Look, he is a vicious murderer and I believe you'll come to see that. I've got the dominoes lined up ready to fall, but he knows it, and East End witnesses have a nasty habit of retracting testimony on the morning of trial. Getting the conviction is more in the balance than I'd like, and it may all come down to you Thomas. You can give me nothing and instead spin things for Danny with your clever words. You can nudge a jury to believe him innocent. Or, with your access to Decker Island, you can find me some nugget that'll make the crucial difference and then get clear, leaving the character whitewash he wants unwritten."

I can feel the frown knotting my forehead. I don't like the extremity of this forced choice.

"There's a third option too," Hughes continues slyly. "You

could help me convict Danny and then finish the book. It'd go flying off the shelves."

"In which case it would never get published," I fire back. "There's the flaw in your argument there."

"You're talking about an autobiography. I mean a biography."

"There's a very clear NDA preventing that."

"And public interest concerns which, in the hands of the right lawyer in front of the right judge, would override an NDA. That can be arranged. You're a clever writer Thomas. It'd be nice to see your name on a cover for once, surely?"

I don't reply, and I can see he thinks he's got to me. Our two coffees arrive at that moment, complete with the bill. Hughes doesn't so much as blink, although I suppose - as Danny would have noted - it's only taxpayers' money he's spending here.

"Listen, just in case it should come to it, I've a unit watching the island. Follow the access to the drawbridge up to where it joins the main road. There's a white Ford in the car park there. The two men inside are my officers. Get to them, any time of night or day, and you'll be safe, understand?"

He downs his drink, places a twenty-pound note on the table, and then is gone with only a nod goodbye. I sip from my own cup and once again my tastebuds sing.

Sing; a hideously appropriate verb. If there's a chance to, do I?

Or even go one step further and commit - in black and white and signed with my name for all the world to see - betrayal?

17.

I'll admit that on Saturday I stormed. Danny wasn't here, Mrs. Canning beat a tactical retreat, and it's why Eric is always uncomfortable in the main house.

Now it's Sunday and I find a strange oasis of calm.

This situation has gone on too long. It's good for no-one, and I believe any resolution of it must be better.

Victim isn't the right word, but too many of the choices that brought us all here weren't mine. That is going to change.

Why Thomas' presence should give me hope I don't know. Is it because he broke through Danny's ice and that opens a prospect of moving forwards? Or is it because he makes this ghost not as alone in the world as I've always felt?

All I'm certain of is that he can be a catalyst.

How strange feeling hope is though. Unaccustomed hope that has sprung to life within me. Enough to turn dark light? That may be stretching it. The pain and its need for release grow too.

I need to back off a bit, take it more slowly. Get my head clear.

Because one way or another I will soon leave Penitent's Isle.

I feel it in my bones. And the consequences be damned.

18.

Am I enjoying the central location of my flat during my weekend off? Am I taking advantage of it to go out on the town wining and dining and fraternising and what have you?

No, I barely did before and I certainly am not now. The various invasions of my privacy needle me all through Saturday, when I was badly out of sorts already.

I dislike Hughes' presumption that I'll eventually help him if he keeps pushing. I also dislike that a policeman has such a clear obsession with getting Danny and Sid behind bars. That said, I believe him about the DNA evidence fingering Danny, whom I reckon capable of such a crime. Nor am I in any doubt about the plausibility of Sid ordering those two killings.

On top of everything else, the idea that Danny wants my wordsmithery to prejudice potential jurors grates badly, because it answers that lingering question of why someone so reticent would engage in autobiography.

And damn Hughes, but that idea of MY name on the cover of MY book as agents and publishers come grovelling to my Canadian or New Zealand mountain lodge for that sensational insider biography of a notorious convicted murderer...well it's a worm inside my head, and the bastard knew exactly what he was doing when he planted it there.

But if we're talking planting things, Danny had my apartment bugged. That's the worse violation. I study my doorframe and notice tiny scuffs in the paintwork near the lock. The desk lamp is slightly out of its normal alignment. A picture hangs not quite horizontally anymore. Someone was indeed in here. I don't look for the microphones because that might arouse suspicion. It's not like they're going to overhear anything interesting anyway.

But knowing they're there infuriates me, as do all the implications thereof. If Danny doesn't trust me then maybe I should damn well just prove myself untrustworthy to him. I sulk away the evening, and decide that if I find clear evidence of any crime I may well pass it on Hughes.

Only clear evidence though, and it partly depends on context, which I need to find out.

On Sunday, as I wake, I get a flashback to that woman who is surely Bella's ghost - she's so like those photos at Sid's house. It's recall rather than real, but it scrambles everything into knots again. It was that electric sensation when I dreamt her touch. I have a weird certainty she could be my missing North Star in life. If she hadn't died twenty-four years ago.

My phone pings. An SMS from Tarquin, who I was literally just about to try contacting. "Metal phobia hitting the proverb Ian. Update the verdant Pk when U can." It baffles me for a full minute before I work it out as 'metaphorical hitting the proverbial', as in shit and fan. Autocorrect wasn't made for people with Tarquin's vocabulary.

I fear it's confirmation there's no way back to my comfortable rut, and only now do I realise how much I'd been hoping for one. Instead my friend has to resort to coded messages and clandestine meetings just to talk to me.

I'm going to have to jump one way or another and pray to land on solid ground. Do I go left and hope Danny keeps opening up, the book does well, and I can haunt some other agency or publisher as a mortgage-paying ghost? Or do I go right and turn spy for Hughes, reaping his promise of a new and better life?

The decision must wait. First I need to get the news and see just how bad where I'm standing is. I text Tarquin back: "11?" He replies: "Yes. Bring nuts."

Union Jacks sprout naturally from the buildings around St. James'. In this part of London tourist attire intermingles with every vainglorious uniform of the British aristocracy, but only the latter have keys to the doors here.

I'll admit I've always been drawn to this exalted little corner of the world that was once the centre of the universe, but today there's an ugliness about it that I put down to my own disenchantment.

When I get to Green Park - as per Tarquin's code - I find a quiet spot among the trees by Lancaster House and remove the packet of peanuts stuffed in my jeans pocket so I can sit down on the grass. Instantly a squirrel descends from a tree and watches.

I open the packet and extract a nut. I stay stock still, but there's little need because it's approaching bold as brass. I can't help thinking that a squirrel is basically a rat with a fancy tail, but how differently we treat it because of that. Quite the metaphor for a good many people who live within a stone's throw of the palace, in fact.

And clearly the East End has got to me already.

The squirrel leans its head over my outstretched palm and grabs the nut. It makes me feel gratifyingly benevolent, until it spits it out and runs off.

"Peanuts won't cut it round here I'm afraid," says Tarquin from behind me. "Try these." He hands me a bag of macadamia nuts from Fortnum and Mason. I don't know if even the rustle of the packet is distinctive, but now four of the rodents are making a beeline for me. Suddenly I don't want them anywhere near, so I hurl a handful of nuts a distance away and stand up.

As a writer I strive to purge redundancy from manuscripts, and that's why there's nothing to ask. Tarquin's expression is answer enough.

"As things stand," he reports, hands clasped behind his back like one of his distinguished ancestors detailing the grisly death of another thousand infantry for no strategic gain, "we're fending off a half-dozen or so investigative journalists who have the scent. Shinelle's in hiding and the agency is rallying behind being quietly appalled at the various suggestions. No-one's ferreted enough to go to print yet, and the hope is some sort of scandal erupts to draw the focus away. The one good thing for all concerned is that your name remains completely out of the picture."

"But Geyser is dead?" I manage.

"The desired outcome is this all fades out and the agency moves on to fight another day. But that only holds as long as we never put out another Shinelle book. I'm sorry."

My face contorts. Tarq has the decency to turn and concentrate on feeding the squirrels instead.

"How's the East End?" he asks over his shoulder.

"It stinks. It all stinks," I reply.

I pass the remainder of the day moodily prowling my bugged bedsit. Then it's time to head east and once again be trapped on Penitent's Isle, awaiting Danny's attentions for the weekdays ahead.

I'm still undecided about everything; who to trust and who to turn on; what it will do to me if Bella's ghost comes to me again; what it will do to me if she doesn't.

The boat's engine was misfiring when we docked, and Eric stayed to fiddle with it, leaving it to Mrs. Canning to bring me my dinner. It's a vegetable lasagna and it smells fantastic. I say as much and take the opportunity to complement her abilities as a cook before she can leave. She smiles, changing her whole persona.

"It's all down to fresh, homegrown ingredients. Eric and his allotment are the ones you want to thank."

"Can I accuse you of false modesty Mrs. Canning?"

"No, you can't. I'll call tomorrow and Eric will collect you as usual. Good night."

It's confirmation that she is, bizarrely, a barrister hired to perform domestic duties.

Her lasagna tastes every bit as good as it smells. But wholesome as their fare may be, Mrs. Canning, Danny and Eric live on money made through extortion. They sent intruders to my flat to install listening devices. They stole audio of forty-eight hours of my life, which must have been deathly boring for someone to sit through.

But I can take revenge through my licence to pry into Danny's life and the lives of those around him.

Even if I don't know to what end, I will ask awkward questions and challenge inadequate answers.

I will get hard.

And should I push too far and things turn nasty, I have backup: two of Hughes' finest parked up twenty-four-seven just a few hundred yards away. True, there's an always-raised drawbridge in between, but at a pinch I could use my key to go out onto the apple tree strand and swim to the shore. My ghost may not be able to cross water, but my body manages a respectable crawl.

And wandering? Here reason resurfaces, urges delay again, and prevails. It's as well I didn't find anything game-changing during my reconnaissance. When I meet Danny tomorrow I'll still be free of any burden of knowing this island's secrets. He did start to talk last week, and that's the better way.

Better for the book because it's attributable rather than spectre conjecture.

Better, if it comes to that, for Hughes and a court of law.

Also, perhaps, better for me, because I don't really know who I am anymore. The electricity of a dreamt woman's touch has somehow blown away the old Thomas, and this new version doesn't seem to be the same servant to inhibition.

But this is a high-risk situation for him to be finding his feet in. Yes, the secret of that second floor is enticing. But spying it out may place me in grave danger.

So patience. Patience.

19.

I was...I suppose some mix between dreading and longing for a visitation last night, but my sleep was dreamless. Danny's looking fatigued this morning too. "Good weekend?" I ask, to start the verbals.

"Tiresome. You?"

"Quiet." I bite back the urge to append that with 'as you know from your bugs'.

"So what's the plan for this week?"

"Pick up where we left off on Friday. I ask you things I judge would help the book. If you don't want to answer then you don't, but there's no taking offence or reprisals."

He nods once. "Go on then."

"So I feel I have some understanding of the context, which is the East End. With Sid...how can I put this? He never really questioned the status quo. The East End was as it was, and he didn't seem to consider the why or how or right or wrong of that. You, on the other hand, have strong arguments and feelings there. I'd like to see those in the book. Do you agree?"

He nods thoughtfully. "You know I'd never considered that about Sid. Yes. I want the history and politics side."

"Good. But there's a maxim when writing which is show don't tell. I think these topics will come up of their own accord, and if we can take the reader to the same destination with hardship or injustice appearing as a natural part of other stories that's the stronger way."

"Meaning you don't want a diatribe?"

"Exactly. And picking up on your use of the word diatribe, I'd like to start on education."

"As in how come an East End oik like me who left school at fourteen knows a word derived from the ancient Greek for lecture?"

"Yes," I say, smiling. I have slightly elongated canine teeth and have been told that I look vampiric when I show them like this. Today that's not bothering me anymore.

Danny eyes me thoughtfully. "At twenty-two the eye injury stopped the one thing I was good at. As you know, Sid took me on, but doing grunt work alongside some right morons. I wanted to think I was better than them, but it occurred to me that if I looked and sounded just like them, had the same cultural references only, and if there was nothing else I could prove I could do, then I wasn't. The only way I could see to fix that was get myself an education."

I nod, genuinely interested. "So how did you go about it?"

"Well, it's a nasty irony in this country that to access an education you need to be educated."

"What do you mean by that?"

"The forms, written applications, references, family friends in academia. Knowing the whole vocabulary of the world of learning. Even where to go and what to ask for. I had none of it. For all I was fit and strong and could beat most people in a fight, with this I was a kid in an adults' world. And with an attitude about it and a prison record to boot."

"And yet you succeeded."

He smiles, and in a warmer way than I've seen to date. "I got lucky. I was helped. There was this town councillor that Sid collected from - this doesn't go in the book by the way. When I say collected from I don't mean cash; with him it was information, instructions from Sid for changes to council projects."

"What makes someone in authority agree to such things?" I wish I could sound less shocked and establishment as I ask this, but today Danny is unfazed.

"Sid set the guy up in a club. Said everyone knew he had a sham marriage; he was a closet pansy and he'd be an easy mark.

He sent this pretty-looking lad who'd do that stuff to pick him up and take him to an apartment they kept for those jobs nearby. Got a nice set of snapshots that would have ruined his career and could have seen him put away, as this was '69 and doing all that with a twenty-year-old was still illegal then."

I recall the photos in the office upstairs, which even the hint of would be rocket fuel for the bestseller lists. I can't get sidetracked though, and right now I don't want Danny to either. "But weren't you saying this was how you got help with an education? You'll have to join the dots for me here."

"Right. So this guy - no names, mind - well, aside from liking boys he was actually a decent bloke. I was the one Sid sent to handle him, and once he accepted how things were he and I got along okay. One day he asked me when I'd left school, then asked why. When I told him he said that door didn't need to be closed. The next week he had some pamphlets for me for college and night school. I probably would have just tossed them or told him to mind his own effing business, but he got me to sit down and helped me through them. I realised this all wasn't as difficult as I'd imagined. It was free too, and there were even grants and so on. He pushed me to choose what I'd like most. I settled on O-Level maths because I hated not being able to do the big sums when I collected. He said he'd put in the application papers for me if I agreed to go for at least the first month."

"Hang on; you wrote your name and address down for someone you were helping extort from?" I don't try to hide my incredulity.

"No-one messed with one of Sid's crew."

"Sid truly had that much power, even over a councillor?" I suppose I should have guessed, but for 'As Nails' he was keen never to spell this out, and I was as keen not to ask.

"Aside from the photos, the man was from the East End.

All his family lived there. He wasn't going to do anything stupid."

I nod slowly in understanding. "So you went?"

"Yes. And once I got past the fear that I was stupid I turned out to be good at academic work. Over the next four years, at college and night school, I got myself seven O-Levels all at top grades and English and history at A-level. I even enrolled in The Open University in '73 and did the first two years of a part-time degree."

Which adds up to 1975, that recurrent date that it's too early to enquire about yet. "I wonder," I say to distract, "if helping you was a tiny way for that councilman to take revenge? Free you with learning and potentially cost Sid one of his best men."

Danny taps a finger to his chin thoughtfully. "Could have been now you say it. I always assumed he fancied me, but that's a cleverer explanation. Either way I owe him."

"Is he still active in politics?" I can't resist asking. It could be someone who's in a senior position now.

"No. Topped 'isself in '71."

And I know why and Danny knows why and both of us knows the other knows it too.

Because it's not all just consequence-free japes and jostling as the movies would have you believe. This is why I didn't want to be involved in it again. Sid's wealth and the wealth of everyone like him - which includes Danny even if there are unusual sides to him - is built on the bones of people's happiness. These hard men impose their hardness on their world, but others who must also live in it can't take it, and they crack apart.

That evening I write everything up. It's actually not bad, and I think he'll eventually agree to include enough of it in some form. Danny's book is less of a chimera than it seemed last week. It might even sell.

Some of it's already out there of course, because he made it part of his boy-done-good persona to open doors to other strata of society in the 80s. By then his desire to learn had switched to finance and those elocution lessons, and his motivations were specific and moneymaking.

But the raw detail of just how intellectually lowly and fragile he was back at the start is aspirational, and really shows another side to his character.

...which is exactly what he wants of course! As Hughes told me. I lose my focus and gnash my teeth for a bit. I wish I could force things to an immediate resolution, but I just have to go at this story's pace and accept its tensions.

Which, by rights, should be tying me in knots, but I've never been so nerveless in my life.

Not until I change for bed and turn off the light. Now I'm all trepidation.

I got no sense at all that Bella was here last night.

If she appears tonight, sparks that contact, my world may explode.

If she doesn't, the bottom may fall out of it.

20.

Where the hell are you Thomas?

I've been standing guard here in the hall the entire night.

You seemed well earlier. Well enough to prise open Danny. All that griping about having to do this, but I reckon he's only gone and started to enjoy talking about himself.

But then why didn't you come once the house was asleep?

You were keen enough to spy last week. What's changed?

Didn't you notice there were no stairs to the top floor?

Surely you can count to three.

So aren't you curious?

About the bit of Penitent's Isle that's still a prison.

21.

It was stomach-turning to wake this morning realising another night had passed uneventfully. There's a seed of doubt now. It's a seed of madness too. Did I merely dream my dream? Am I misremembering its incredible potency? I'm petrified that this might be true.

I gather myself and force focus onto the waking day. I retain my new resolve, but there's a hint of brittle fragility that wasn't there yesterday.

Still tacking either side of 1975-to-1979, I steer today's session into the 1980s. British ruling class prejudice against the East End reared its head more than once yesterday, so my question to Danny is what changed?

He shrugs. "Thatcher."

I tilt my head inquiringly.

"The establishment didn't know how to handle her. They'll get all the reins of power back one day, you watch, but for a while she made how much you were earning more important than coats of arms and who daddy was."

"Meritocracy you mean?"

He shakes his head. "Not really, but as close as England's every likely to get. I was lucky too though. I had a share of several businesses right on the borders between East and West. Restaurants, clubs, even a couple of art galleries. Real estate too. Suddenly the line where things got fashionable was moving, and for every place I was cashing in on I was buying two more on the next street east. I knew the people and the areas and hardly anyone else I was competing with had a clue.

I even became fashionable myself, and you can screw all sorts of profit out of that too."

Naturally I try to hone in on specific people and instances, but that's where the shutters start coming down. Unlike the long-gone bars and clubs of the 1960s that Sid's gang used to collect from, the characters in these stories are still present and occupying positions of influence. Quite a few probably occupy pages of that folio of compromising photos too. Whatever Danny's reason for doing this autobiography is, it doesn't trump the value of these assets. Thus, forty minutes later, I'm midway through getting nowhere fast when Mrs. Canning knocks, opens the door, and shoots Danny a 'come quickly' look.

He leaves, and just minutes later I hear the faint sound of the drawbridge going down then up again.

Mrs. Canning reappears, her face a little flushed.

"Unfortunately Mr. Decker's needed on a business matter and I doubt he'll be back today. I'll take you over to the cottage now."

"How long have you lived here on the island, Mrs. Canning?" I ask as we cross the gravel.

She gives me a look that's somewhere between scornful and amused. "I have no comment, Thomas."

"Of course," I reply. Then she's gone and I try to work out a way to structure the morning's nebulous mist of hints into something which is both interesting to the reading public and unlikely to attract influential ire or libel suits.

I fail.

And I don't even care that I fail.

What matters is Bella's ghost, and she's forsaken me.

For a moment I contemplate wandering to the main house, but it would be downright dangerous to leave my body feeling like this.

It's the flesh-and-blood form of the sadness.

The only time it's ever been this bad before was during those months of no replies about my novel from agents and publishers.

Back then the prospect of tomorrow still exerted a grip. Now, if Bella's gone or was never even real, there's only a yawning void there.

And it's terrifying.

22.

A pirate king would have come.

Even a bloody cat would have come. They're curious.

What he's getting won't make a book. So, what? Just leave it at that? Pathetic. That's so half-hearted. Go use your talents to snoop, spy!

I've a mind to go over there and jam my whole hand right into his face to see if the shock happens again and wakes him up from his dreary trudge through however many months he's got left.

I don't dare though. I still don't know what that electricity was. It did something to me when I touched him. It was...

Okay, fine: I'm curious too. There! Happy?

But I'm exhausted from standing guard.

And scared, yes.

Obviously. When I've tried so hard to keep myself together for so many years and that spark felt like it would blow me apart.

It all makes me angry. Which is alright because that's something to hold onto. It'll serve as rope and anchor for now.

I'll wait in the hall again.

Surely tonight...?

23.

I awake.

Nothing. Again. No Bella.

I've never felt so alone in my life.

What was with all that getting hard bullshit of mine?

Shelled creatures that leave their shells die bad deaths in no time flat. Nature has iron laws about this.

What the hell was I thinking?

Her ghost doesn't exist. She never existed.

Nor will this book. If this was 1997 instead of 2003 maybe, but Tarquin was right: it's a dying genre. To recapture the attention it would have to be sensational, and if that's even out there Danny's not going to give it to me. He doesn't WANT this book. So where's the desire for it going to come from?

Not from me, I can tell you that. My inkwell is dry.

Everything is grey and unappealing.

I stare into space for God knows how long until there's a knock at the door and Mrs. Canning is there. She seems concerned by what she reads in my eyes, but she says nothing beyond: "Unfortunately Mr. Decker will be away today and tomorrow too. It's more convenient that you return home for the time being. Assume the same routine for Sunday night to be ready to start on Monday. If not I'll call with alternative arrangements."

I'm indifferent. "Sure." I trudge robotically out the gate behind her to where Eric and his boat wait.

The sky is grey. The industrial sprawl and consumer waste filth all around is grey. The Thames is grey. It could be the Styx. If Eric wants Charon's Obol I'll give it to him. Leaving this all behind would be only relief.

24.

Danny got home in the small hours. Mrs Canning coming to watch over me woke me up, although I went right back to sleep as it's been an exhausting week of long nights.

When I go to him the next morning he's in his gym pummelling his punchbag.

"Hi."

"Morning."

"Everything okay?"

He smacks the bag with a vicious right uppercut. "It's the last time that one tries to be a smart arse."

"Who?"

"You know it's better you don't know names."

I glare at him, but actually I played for this little upper hand. "Have you found anything out from Thomas then?"

He screws up his face. "No. I don't know how. He just flips everything back onto me."

"No bad trait in an autobiography ghostwriter, one might say."

"Yeah, alright." He hits the bag again. "But he's steering clear of Sid either out of genuine loyalty or because he wants to seem loyal to me. How do I turn that around to pumping him for information about something so personal to the old bastard?"

"I don't know! Human-to-human conversation is hardly my speciality, is it? This is why you hired him though."

He snorts and shakes his head, and I can see that if I push this further it'll just rile him.

"Danny, there's one more thing." How much should I tell him? I'm very conflicted about this.

"Hm?"

"You can't trust Thomas."

His face hardens. "What makes you say that?"

Because he's a ghost and I saw him sneak into your study? I can't tell Danny this because I'm afraid of what he'd do to Thomas...and I can't lose Thomas. For all that I'm furious at him right now, I need to know he's there in the world. The alternative would be...unbearable.

"It's just a feeling. But please be careful, okay?"

Now he grins a shark's grin. "Come on! I'm always careful, aren't I?"

25.

Wednesday through to Friday was all awful fog. I slept on the bed sofa in sofa mode and sat for hours staring vacantly on it in bed position. On Saturday morning my dubious sanity finally seems to latch onto some psychological trail of breadcrumbs that leads in an actual direction.

I don't believe in Danny's book. I may complete it and I may get paid for it, but it will kill what dregs remain of my career. I need a complete reboot, and nothing on Penitent's Isle is going to provide that.

Thus to Hughes.

And to an uncomfortable realisation.

The more I want that new life and new start far away, the more I realise it won't be given to me cheaply or easily. The string on the lure will keep pulling it further and further away if I reach for it.

Ultimately, to get what he's offering I'll have to produce the goods. Taking stock, the guns can't be burnt like paper so would be found in a raid so have no value. They may well be legal anyway. The cash is to be expected and the shareholdings are likely legitimate, even if how they were obtained perhaps had elements of coercion. All of which equals nothing.

Will Danny tell me anything important enough for my second-hand testimony of it in a court of law to prove crucial? It's unlikely, and also it would doubtless be painted as embittered and/or bribed treachery by his lawyer. I doubt jurors would be impressed by that kind of turncoatery.

So that leaves two prospects, the first of which is, what could Hughes do with detailed knowledge of the contents of that extortion folder? Without the photographs themselves, which I can't get because they're in a locked cabinet behind a locked door on a floor of the house I'm not allowed on, precious little. What would he do with it even if I could get the photos? Some of the great and the good of the country are in there, but would Hughes want to bring them to justice for their crimes? On this score I believe Danny, and that's a flat no. Realistically, I can't use this.

It therefore all comes down to finding that watch, 'World's Best Cleaner', which my testimony can link to Sid and the day after the two murders. He's likely to be absent, holed up in his Spanish villa fighting off extradition, so any denial would be weak indeed.

I know narrative. I know hook. I know story. This would work. And it's the only thing which does.

It's even the truth, coincidentally.

And I still believe it's out there.

On both Thursday and Friday mornings an odd thing happened on my phone: an SMS message appeared, and then ten minutes later, before I got round to opening it, it disappeared as if it had never existed. A ghost message.

It happens again today, and this time I do open it. "Same place as last time. CU there ASAP if OK."

I sigh and get my coat.

Today Hughes is already at Mork & Stark waiting for me, and fending off a young, trendy couple who want to share his nook.

"Morning Thomas. Good to see you out and about again. Nice bird that waitress. Remembered the fancy coffee you like."

I manage the barest of facial twitches by way of reply.

"Been a hard two-day week has it?" Hughes smirks.

"I'd just like to know where I stand."

"Well what's on the table is the same as it's always been Thomas. I'd like to know where you stand too."

"I think there's one little thing - an object - that might link Sid, Danny and the two murders. I haven't found it yet, but if I'm able to I reckon it would stick in a jury's heads and make the crucial difference."

Hughes smiles. Quite a sickening, almost insane smile. "That's exactly the sort of thing I'm after. Are you going to tell me what?"

"Not until I've found it. I'd also want specifics for our deal at that point."

"You don't trust the word of The Met?"

"I'm a writer. I prefer to see things in black and white."

He pretends more offence than I think he's taken. "Thomas you should know better than to be a doubter. Your cosy childhood in Dorset was taxpayer-funded, remember?"

"What?" I'm completely nonplussed.

"Your dad never said?"

"Said what? I have no idea what you're talking about."

Hughes shakes his head. "You don't really think all that money for the house came from flogging Hi-Fi on commission? And he was a lousy salesman."

I blink and gape. "I was only six when he died," I mumble eventually. Mother rarely talked about him when I was small because it would make both of us cry. By the time I got old enough Geoff was always there, and he hated being reminded that her love for him would never be half as strong.

Hughes sees something that makes him soften. "It must have been hard on you. So you genuinely don't know?"

"Apparently not," I rasp out.

"He had the most amazing knack for finding secrets out for me. Wouldn't say how he did it, and I was never able to discover his trick. Everything he ever sold me checked out though. I have to say I was gutted when he died." He studies me. "I suspected foul play you know. I mean who goes to sleep and never wakes up at twenty-nine years old and no drink or pills involved? It was only a few weeks before the trial and your dad had some new theory that sounded like he might be onto something big. I wondered if they'd found out what he knew and poisoned him somehow. Nothing showed up in the autopsy though." He pauses. "At least nothing we could trace with the science back then."

"The trial...them. Do you mean...?" My throat dries shut.

"That's right Thomas. Your good friends Sid Marsh and Danny Decker."

26.

This time I'm set like stone on the boat ride. I don't even notice the swaying or the rising stink of the East End. I go in and unpack my things. Then I wait until Eric has brought the meal Mrs. Canning has prepared. I leave it untouched; I only waited this long to ensure I won't be disturbed. I lie on the bed and in seconds am wandering.

My fury in ghost form remains ice cold. I go directly to the main house...but I rein myself in on the ground floor.

Yes I want to know what's up there. Yes I want to find that

watch. But is rushing it the best way? There's a new problem now which is that if I find out this truth about Danny I won't be able to speak a word to him without my hatred being obvious. He would want an explanation. Without one I don't believe he'll let me walk off this island. But with one I'd be signing my death warrant twice over.

It is necessary to wait.

So instead of going up there I try to appease my livid ghost by finally perusing Danny's library.

There are some carefully-inked names of previous owners in the beautiful antique volumes. In 'Wuthering Heights', which by the foxing has been read more times than anything else here, I'm intrigued by the neat copperplate-handwriting: 'F.W.Eurich, Little Germany, Bradford, 1882.' Why does or did Bradford contain a Little Germany? This inscription was written only 34 years after Emily - my favourite of the Brontës - died. Howarth isn't that far from Bradford, so perhaps reader and author met?

I extricate myself from the book. Of course they didn't meet. This most brilliant of authors had to use a man's name instead of her own to get published. She barely left her village during her lifetime, which was ended aged thirty by tuberculosis. Victorian Yorkshire was another vicious, hard place where death came too young.

I suppress another surge of anger, and force my ghost to return to its physical self.

27.

Thomas almost glowed in the library. Something in him is changed.

I resolved yesterday that I was done with passivity. No more waiting and guard duty.

I give him a two hour head start. When I arrive at the cottage he is just getting changed for bed. I study his naked form. Even as a ghost it affects me. Were I whole I'd be in trouble, because I know what my response to his lean, rangy body would be. Like Baskerville, he's very much my type. It's a disappointment when he pulls on pyjamas.

He spins and flails. When he stretches he's too tall for the duvet and his feet stick out. Finally he falls asleep, but only to toss and turn. He's troubled by something, this ghost.

"Hughes," he mutters.

Did he spot the rozzers on the bank from the boat? Is he wondering how to bring their handler's name into the conversation?

That swine of a copper's faked evidence meant Danny was locked away when Bella finally abandoned her body. Hughes' name did come up on the Wednesday of Thomas' first week, I remember. Danny kept his cool and even opened up for a bit afterwards, but when Thomas left he had to go upstairs and beat the shit out of his punchbag until his hands started to bleed.

"Brontë. Emily Brontë."

Thomas says it like a mumbled version of 'Bond. James Bond.'

"Eurich."

How can he know that?!

How can he possibly know the name that's written in my copy of Wuthering Heights? I've watched him the whole time his body's been in the library with Danny, and although I could see he wanted to touch the books, he never has.

His spectral form went right into it earlier of course, but...unless this writer's spirit can somehow read a closed book in the darkness?!

It's the only explanation, even if I've no idea how he

manages it.

If I could learn that trick I could read the bridge code.

Or, much easier, Thomas could read the code!

It's the sensation of a cold sweat. How can I make him do it? What does he want that I could offer in exchange? What are my options for communicating with him?

"World's best cleaner," he sighs suddenly, before groaning and shifting again.

That's what's etched on the back of that mannish old watch, but she never takes it off, so how does he know? Maybe he read it the same way he read the name in the book.

The same way he could read the code.

It could set me free.

Free to finally leave Penitent's Isle.

If that's what I truly want.

28.

I wake up rotated on the bed and knotted in sheets.

Bella's ghost haunted the edge of my scrambled dreams all night. It churns my insides like a rollercoaster. I wanted this so much. I have no appetite and can find no focus to begin my day.

Because she must be a hallucination. Did I not step back from madness only thanks to that realisation? Last week's cliff-edge to nothingness is suddenly back full force. To follow her, as I ache to do, would rob me of the revenge I now seek. That price would be insignificant were she only real, but she's not. She's not! I wish these delusions would leave me alone. I hate knowing these depths.

I have to get outside these walls, so I dress and use my key to unlock the gate.

But if anything her ghost is more present here. I walk the

triangular path and I feel desperate and futile and trapped, and she whispers into my head 'Yes. Exactly.' I retreat back inside just to try and get away from it.

I was up much earlier than I realised, and that gives me time to calm down in. My goal of finding that watch anchors me, lets me separate out a portion of my head where wishful thinking and rational analysis can coexist in a temporary detente.

Is the woman in my visions definitely Bella? Yes; I recognise her face from the photos Sid had.

Is there any way she could be real?

Obviously I have to be more open to that possibility than your typical non-wanderer. That said, in all my out-of-body travels I have never once seen a trace of another ghost. Does that mean they don't exist on some other level? No, but I just have this certainty that if one were there when I left my body I would be able to perceive them...

Unless that ghost was hiding from me.

I dive into retrospect and as soon as I look for it it's immediately clear; I've been feeling eyes on me since I first set foot here. The clock in the hallway when I wandered, the staircase bookshelf in the study. It's distinctly felt like they were watching me, so perhaps they were.

Is that the secret? Does Bella's ghost venture out before returning to haunt the second floor?

But I saw a light there. Ghosts don't need light.

And that feeling of being observed could well be nothing more than the walls and the architecture and the security and Mrs. Canning and Eric and Danny.

There's a way to find out though. To hell with playing facial expression chess with Danny and tic-tac-who-knows-what and all my earlier caution. I resolve that right here and right now I will lay my body down and my ghost will visit that second floor. The ramifications will be as they will be. I must seek Bella's ghost immediately. I have to, or I'll go mad.

Then, of course, the bloody phone rings, and like a true Englishman I feel obligated to answer it.

I arrive in Danny's study in bullish mood. I want all this out of the way fast so I can go wandering. I am prepared to break china.

Once we're seated and have done the brief, obligatory pleasantries, I don't even hesitate.

"Danny, as you know, complex stories are about threads and the drama comes from the places those weave together. The degree you gave up; your engagement to Bella after years of admiring her hopelessly from afar; a new distance between you and Sid that only got wider; the death of an informant and a policeman, blown up in a car by a hand grenade. All these strands knot together at one point in time. Let's talk about 1975."

He freezes, and I'd swear the bookshelf with the stairs hidden behind it holds its breath.

"It's not that easy, Thomas," he growls finally. "There's a code."

"The East End code of silence you mean?"

"Yes."

"Which I interpret as meaning you know who killed Detective Constable Brian Hughes and Terry Norris but you can't say."

His flat, unblinking stare with its threat of imminent violence meets mine for an aeon. "What I can tell you, again, is that I did not kill those two men."

"I believe you," I say. And I'm surprised to realise that I do.

"But I was reading a newspaper at the weekend and I spotted something that could make all of this topical rather than historical. What do you know about Part 10 of the Criminal Justice Act 2003?"

I'm watching for his reaction, but again it's only ice stare.

"Thomas, if you have something to say just say it without pissing about."

"Fine. That Act removes the double jeopardy block on a retrial for a serious crime such as murder."

"If there's new evidence."

"Yes."

"So?"

"So aren't you worried Hughes might have some? I assume those are his men in the car park over in Rainham Marshes. Eric keeps me in a fogged up cabin on the boat so they can't see me clearly. And why send me by boat in the first place? Why not the much easier drawbridge? I get the impression you're under siege here."

Suddenly Danny laughs. Not in a friendly or comforting way, but it's finally actual rapport of a sort.

"I'm impressed Thomas. I see why you're good at your job. Don't worry though. Hughes and his ilk are always circling the likes of me because I'm a barrow-boy done good and that upsets their worldview. That's all."

"Is it?"

His jaw tightens. "Meaning?"

I sigh tightly, but it's faked because I don't care about the clear tension. "I'm on delicate ground here because I'm also bound by a code."

"Sid?" Danny's there instantly.

"Yes." I pause to project dilemma; if you're going to voice a convenient lie to erase a number of awkward secrets then ham that porky-pie up! "There was this one thing he said at the end of a day when we'd been talking about the Hughes-Norris murders and he'd been protesting his complete lack of knowledge. It stuck with me because he got so vehement."

Several muscles are going in different parts of Danny's face. I make him wait. Then I do the accent slightly. Just enough to bring Sid's ghost into the room.

"I call 'im world's best cleaner but 'e only goes and leaves the fuckin' pineapple pin lying there."

"And your interpretation of that is?" Now you can hear that Danny's an East End boy at heart. I'm ninety percent sure he recognised the watch inscription.

"Assuming pineapple means grenade, then my interpretation is that Sid ordered someone to kill those two and that person left the pin of the murder weapon at the scene. That Sid was so angry can only mean the police found it."

"Thomas, I was put on trial for those murders, remember? A grenade pin was never listed in evidence."

"Why would it be when there were shards of the actual grenade embedded all through the wreckage of the car? The pin didn't prove anything that wasn't already known."

"Okay. Then your point is what exactly?"

"It didn't prove anything in 1975. Assuming the police still have that pin, does twenty-first-century DNA technology, which can finger a person from a microscopic fragment of skin or sweat, show something previously unknown? If so it could be the evidence that justifies a retrial under the new law."

Danny leans back in his chair, but his relaxation is an act. I spot the slight tremor in his hand. A desperate little part of my brain alerts me that I should be getting very scared, but I blank it. I only care about getting out of this room so I can search for Bella.

"I don't know if Mrs. Canning said, but I only had half an hour free today. I think that's about up, so let's end this here."

We rise eagerly together and he shows me out of the door. As I walk down the hallway I hear him leave the study and turn right, moving swiftly towards Mrs. Canning's apartment.

I'm free. And now it's back across the gravel and to the single thing that matters to me anymore.

29.

Thomas, Thomas, Thomas.

Who knew you had that in you?

I did. The pirate king is stirring. I saw him there from the first moment I looked upon your true face.

From the speed of his walk back to the cottage I know he's coming to find me. I don't know how I know this. I don't know how he can even know about me. But I'm certain.

What are his reasons though?

And what is it I want?

Danny and Mrs. Canning are closeted, that new snippet of information from Sid's ghost fretting the both of them. They'll be hours. When Danny's car doesn't leave Eric will know there's stress going on. He'll be hiding out in his potting shed until nightfall.

So it's just me and Thomas.

I wait at the top of the stairs in full view.

I see the subtle shift in the patterns of the light as he enters through the closed door.

He's halfway up the stairs before he spots me and stops dead.

I beckon him. He follows. I'm glad we're both mute in this state. If I could speak I'm not sure I'd be able to, and that'd look weak.

We could go straight up a wall and through the floor, but I want him to know where the stairwell is hidden so I go to the smallest of the empty bedrooms and through its false wardrobe so we can ascend the conventional way. I don't do a tour, but as we go down the hall we pass enough doorways for him to see I have everything any captive could desire.

There's a music room with concert-grade instruments I never play.

A gym, which was a mistake from day zero - as we both know, it's hardly as if your blood runs in my veins, Danny.

A many-cushioned TV lounge where I can hurl myself in fits of tantrum.

The schoolroom tutors from far afield used to be smuggled into. Mrs. Canning would tell them I had a rare condition that stopped me from going into sunlight. I do: Danny's and my own paranoia. Which has its origin in pain.

At the end of the corridor the best light comes in from the east-facing day room with its balcony and views. It's where I read and write and wither away. It's where I've left my corpse, which we have need of now.

He sees my physical form and his face is a Munch painting of shock. What did he think I was? Ghosts have no need to sit so I don't direct him to a chair. I take one last look at him standing frozen, and then I return to my body.

When the haze clears from my vision I sit upright on the chaise-longue. "I'm Cathy," I say. "I can't see you anymore."

I wonder if he has some clever way of communicating like his reading trick, but either he doesn't or he's still dumbstruck.

I place a metronome on the coffee table he was standing next to. "It's easy to move. Your right for yes, left for no. Show me yes so I know you understand."

I wait but there's nothing. Surely he hasn't gone?

I separate again. I rarely try to do it this quickly, and it's a frustrating struggle. It takes me a full five minutes. Then I'm free and I can see him. He wafts his hand through the metronome and shrugs helplessly. I reach forward and flick it left then right. It's practically effortless. He tries it again with a concentrated frown on his face, but achieves nothing.

I go once more to my body. This is a complete pain in the arse and it's giving me a vicious headache, but it's the frustration more than anything else because I'm aching to connect with him.

And doesn't that ache just capture my story?

I can't stay trapped any longer. It has to end because it's unbearable. Thus I return to my original plan, because I can only work out what I do next from a place of freedom.

"Two questions in sequence," I say to the blank air in front of me, my voice harsh with strain. "I'll leave my body to see your replies. First, you can read something written even on a closed page, is that correct? Second, will you promise to read something for me if I tell you who the world's best cleaner is?"

I lie back again and this time it takes me seven infuriating minutes. His face is solemn and unreadable. I hold up one finger and in reply he nods. Thought so. Good! Now I raise two ghostly digits. There's a slight pause and I wonder why, because he's clearly fixated on that phrase enough to say it in his sleep, but again he nods.

I worm back into my heavy flesh again. "Useful trick," I croak. I so wish I could see him. Instead, trying to keep my voice even, I tell him, "In the gatehouse there's a locked room with the drawbridge control. There's a grubby desk in there. Tucked under the lamp on it is a piece of paper with the code to open the bridge. Eric's poor at remembering numbers you see. I want that code. Go back to the promontory shore at four this afternoon when it's low tide and draw it in the mud. You won't be able to see me but I'll be there to read it. In return, world's best cleaner is Mrs. Canning. It's engraved on her watch."

30.

I wanted to stay near her with all my soul, but the sadness was coming on badly and she'd defined the next step.

I awake completely confused, and my biological self descends into a welter of physical stress symptoms to spin everything into a vortex.

She's real. She's corporeal. But also a ghost. She has the same two halves that I do. Until you realise there's another like you you have no idea the extent to which you crave that. No idea.

And she's Cathy, not Bella. There is a strong resemblance, but they were never the same person.

Who is Cathy though? Whilst she might live up there in gilded luxury, I believe she is a prisoner here.

Having to communicate in such a laborious manner was infuriating. I want to talk to her all day and night. Sleep and food would be annoying irrelevances; my need to know her is so much greater.

But focus. Keep piecing the facts together. What is she to Danny that he keeps her here like this?

And Mrs. Canning? The world's best cleaner surely knows about Cathy. Does she also know how it feels to pull the pin from a grenade and throw it through the window of a parked car with two men inside? A time may return where I can care about that, but she and Hughes and Danny and Sid and everything else in the filthy and knotted tapestry of the human world can go hang.

It's ten to one. Lunch will arrive inconveniently soon. I have no appetite, but it's better to be present for the knock at the door. Only after that will I be able to undertake Cathy's task.

But what was that catch in her voice when she asked it of me? Foreboding. A portent. I'm out of my depth in this, and now I suddenly have so very, very, very much to lose.

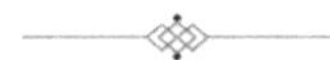

Lunch was late, and lunch was unusually basic and a little burnt.

Wrapping up Hughes' information as a Sid moment that can't be checked plus my own deduction has clearly set the cat amongst the pigeons. Did I overreach? Perhaps, but do you know what, I enjoyed it. I felt...hard. That's the word for it! All my life my vision has been sideways like that of a deer, scanning for threats and perennially nervous. Today I became a tiger. I earned my stripes. I saw only what I was hunting, and the feeling was glorious.

What Cathy asked me to find out was simple. The code is 1503.

Why does that ring a bell? The date on that blank birth certificate in Danny's office. The 15th of March. 1503. Coincidence? I doubt it. 1976 was the year. If the date relates to Cathy it would make her twenty-seven.

Every time I re-realise that the woman literally of my dreams is real and so close my heart does somersaults. My lifelong training in detached and diffident pragmatism has left me utterly unprepared to deal with this.

This: I don't even know what this is.

But of course I also do. I read don't I? It's the elixir we all crave that writers through the ages have sought to bottle in sentences. It's bolt-from-the-blue, logic-defying love. It's the divine madness even the gods envy. Overwhelming, obsessive, all-consuming love.

I have no other reason left.

I only want Cathy.

I need Cathy.

At four O'clock sharp I am standing where the grass dissolves into Thames. I'm certain I can feel her presence. My soul thrums in response, but I'm scared of what I'm about to hand over.

For a fleeting moment I consider holding it back until I can understand its significance. But to what end? To set myself up with a lever of control over her? That's not love. Love requires respect and love requires trust. Love does not confer the right to judge.

I bend down and, with my index finger, draw 1503 in the muck.

Suddenly the numbers blur as if a palm has erased them. One too impatient to wait for the tide, even though it has already turned.

Electricity! Her touch. The same blinding, wonderful sensation I felt on Wednesday morning the week-before-last.

Then she is gone, for I feel her ghost near me no more.

31.

In the space of a few hours Thomas has solved the riddle that's trapped me here for years. 1503, my birthday for crying out loud! Okay, the system locks you out after five wrong tries, and all three of my fellow islanders get furious when that happens, but if I'd kept at it would I not have guessed right sooner or later?

It makes me dwell on whether I've truly ever wanted to leave. It's complex; isn't that the catch-all for such situations?

And now there's Thomas. I couldn't resist brushing his hand again. What is that glorious, glorious sensation when we touch? How does it reshape everything around it?

He felt it too. I'm certain. I'm glad he didn't talk. His prowess with language would get in the way. His face is less wordy and more eloquent. He looked right at me, and in his eyes...

To be wanted like that! To be wanted for who and what I am rather than as a legacy of lost love!

This is why I need to absent myself from here for a while. Just so I can see things from a distance and try to work them out. The worry has always been that, if free to, I will turn away from my body as Bella did and the connection will break.

But that's not going to happen now, and I can and will prove it. There's a thrill running through me that unites my two halves. Three doesn't work in the Thomas and me equation I'm contemplating. Two pairs of our two parts makes an even four, the square on a dice. I've never needed my physical incarnation more.

And yet now I lay it down and bid its eyes closed so I can take my leave.

I'm scared to part from it, and I absolutely love this new feeling.

Will I venture as far as Purfleet or simply roam the marshes? I don't know yet. I just want to be able to cross the water and look at Penitent's Isle from the outside. Then return and show them that now I will always come back.

And for all my certainty I want to prove that to myself too.

Three minutes later I'm out. I go through the floor because it's more direct. Then the big stairs down to the ground floor. Danny and Mrs. Canning are still in session. Normally I would listen in on something this important, but not today.

Eric is weeding his carrot patch. Will he be able to get inside and stop the drawbridge when he hears it? It takes twenty-four seconds to lower into position. He's kneeling on the ground with his hands covered in soil and his reaction time isn't what it used to be. I don't think he'll make it.

I go into the cottage and through the locked door. Sucking

energy from the air I focus it on my spectral index finger and go poltergeist on the keypad four times. 1. 5. 0. 3.

I'm rewarded with the sound of clanking. I go out through the stone wall and wait as the rectangle of daylight grows agonisingly slowly.

Eric looks up and around, mouth open. It's a full eight seconds before he gets to his feet. Danny bursts from the main house and reaches the gatehouse ahead of him. Mrs Canning appears at the front door, her eyes roving suspiciously.

But none of them can see me like this. None of them can touch me or contain me. They know this. It's why they have their routine: Mrs. Canning, sitting next to me upstairs, confirms I'm awake and therefore in my body. She radios this to Danny and Eric, and only then is the bridge lowered for the car to drive out. I think Thomas can get clear of his body a lot faster than I can, but even he would never make it across before they raise the thing again.

Today the tables are turned. The lock on the control room door takes longer than they have, and as the bridge drops the last few feet to connect with the land and remove the unbreachable barrier of water I'm already rushing over it. I only stop when I reach the shore, turning to look back.

The bridge begins to move upwards, but then stops and lowers again.

They know I've gone.

They still have my body, but they don't have the part of me that matters.

I wish I could ease their distress. Tell them they don't need to worry anymore. I'm not going to go too far or too long away like Bella did when Danny was locked up in prison.

Another ghost has changed everything. I'd return to Penitent's Isle anyway, but a thousand times more because Thomas is there.

32.

The rumble of the drawbridge is a rare enough sound that I still notice it. When I hear feet running fast over the gravel I shudder at what I've done. Cathy's used the code. She's escaping Penitent's Isle.

A short while later the cottage's front door opens and Mrs. Canning is eyeing me.

"Good afternoon," I say smoothly. "Is everything alright?"

"Of course."

"Does Danny want to see me?"

She's blinking and off-guard. Her blouse is a little askew and I see the glint of gold at her wrist. I seize my opportunity.

"By the way, is that a Smith's Imperial watch? My grandfather always said they were the finest British timepiece ever made."

Mrs. Canning frowns, confused. There's no way I could have seen the make from the sliver of watch visible below her sleeve, but she's distracted; Cathy's doing.

"Yes. And your grandfather was right. Mr Decker gave it to me."

"That was most generous of him."

She shakes her head clear. "Please stay inside here," she says. As she leaves the cottage I hear her lock the door behind her.

It's all I can do not to laugh out loud. In the space of a minute the woman who prides herself on revealing nothing has revealed that Danny is both a liar and a murderer, and that interesting things are happening outside.

Where I can still go effortlessly. I sit back in my chair, close my eyes, and am out through the wall and close enough behind her to hear Danny's snarled "Well?"

"He's in there. I've locked the door."

"Keep it that way. He knows something. This is no coincidence."

Only now does it dawn on me that I'm in considerable danger. What was it Danny said about Sid and Bella? "She was forbidden territory though. Cross Sid on that score and you'd wind up in The Thames with a pair of concrete boots. We all knew that."

And once the synaptic dominoes start falling they topple en masse. Is Cathy Bella's daughter? 1976 was three years before Bella died. That plus the resemblance says an obvious yes. Making Danny her father? Between Sid's and Danny's murderous vigilance anything else is impossible. But I'm cast-iron certain Sid is unaware he has a granddaughter.

Suddenly I'm very, very afraid. Did I leave my brain behind when I started playing hard?! Danny is a confirmed killer and I've interfered with that which is most precious to him.

The drawbridge mechanism grinds. Danny swears and rushes to the gatehouse door. "Eric! Leave it down," he shouts inside. "She has to be able to get back in."

So he knows Cathy is a ghost and that she can't cross water. More neurons join up in my brain. He bought this place in 1979, the same year Bella died. No-one knows how she died, but is that because people don't know about ghosts? I do. I know about the sadness. I know what can happen if the spirit stays out of the body for too long. 1983 he moved here. I was seven when I started to wander. Did Cathy show the signs at the same age? Did Danny move to Penitent's Isle because it was the only place in all of East London he could keep his young daughter trapped near her body?

As he crunches back across the gravel Danny's face is a mixture of livid and utterly desperate. "Sit by her," he instructs Mrs. Canning. Radio the instant she wakes up. The old woman nods. "The bridge stays down until you get the call," Danny commands Eric, who's followed him. "Then raise it whether I'm back or not, and keep it raised. In the meantime change the code. And don't fucking write it down this time."

"You're going out?" Mrs. Canning's question rescues Eric from Danny's glare.

"Yes. If she's there she can see and hear me. I need to try and bring her home."

"Hughes' men will see you," Mrs. Canning cautions. "Wandering around aimlessly yelling at the air won't be a good look."

"Do you think I give a fuck?" he shouts. Then he strides off out through the gate to cross the bridge to the marshes.

His fear for Cathy infects me. Might she never return to her body? The thought is chilling. I can't lose her. I was so keen not to judge or to control, but did I err? Danny is sharp and Danny is competent. If he upended his whole life to move here for Cathy's protection then he must have had good reason.

I may not be able to talk to Cathy or she to me like this, but I can see her. If I can find her out there I can beckon her to return.

Just come back to your body Cathy.

We can take everything else from there.

Please don't stay away too long and come apart. I simply couldn't bear that.

You'd be killing me too.

33.

I don't go far, nor do anything much. It's enough to be on unfamiliar ground, where I lie on the grass and gaze skywards. The birds know when a ghost is here, but after a time they become used to me and resume the cheeping and fluttering of their lives.

Penitent's Isle is the only home I've ever known. Danny did try to make it otherwise, but I lasted less than a week at a Swiss school aged ten. I liked the place and the other girls. What scared me was the decreasing claim my body had on me.

We tried twice more in later years, but each time I begged Danny never to send me away again, and finally he agreed. I told him I would take leave of the world like Bella did. I knew exactly what that would do to him. And what it would make him do to me.

Bella. Why don't I call her Mum? I guess it's because you earn that title, and she never could. Why don't I call Danny Dad? He's done more than his share of parenting, but...

I don't blame Bella. She didn't have it in her because I don't think she ever got the chance to. Her own mother, Laoise, had her when she was just nineteen. Sid saw her singing in a nightclub, and Irish or not he just had to have her. He showered her with glittering diamonds, fancy clothes and the best of everything that money and fear could acquire. He kept her like a caged bird. A pretty doll to drape on his alpha arm. She who had sung so sweet that hard-bitten men wiped a tear from their eye. He left her with no control over any part of her life.

Laoise pushed Bella away because Bella bound her to an existence she hated and sought the bravery to escape. Could Laoise leave her body too? I believe she probably had the talent, but from the little I know of her fiercely Catholic upbringing she probably avoided it as one of the thousand Satanic pathways the religious are made terrified to tread. So in the end she went outside herself the one time only that I know of, aged twenty-four and in a traditionally mortal and chemically-induced manner involving a bottle of sleeping pills.

Danny says Bella began to detach after that. Places and people she remembered from her travels made it possible to work out the years. She never told Sid or anyone else. Just terrified herself and kept it all bottled up. Then 1975, and by the time I arrived she'd already half gone and it was only a matter of when the rest would follow.

I'm sorry Bella. I wish I'd known you. I wish I'd learned to call you Mum.

Did Sid ever realise? Did he ever guess at my existence? That's what we hoped Danny could find out via Thomas.

But am I similarly-fated to my mother and grandmother? I've lived under the shadow of that fear my whole life, but do you know what? I believe I'm not. I no longer want to die like they did. I want to live. I want the physical things in life. I want Thomas. I want him as he is, and I want to watch him become all he can be.

"Cathy!"

Danny's hoarse shout scares the birdlife and snaps me out of my reverie.

"Whatever you want love. Just come home. Cathy! Please. I'm sorry."

I'm mortified that I've reduced him to apology. He deserves so much better for all he's done.

"It's okay Danny. You don't need to fear for me now. We've all been stuck, all of us on Penitent's Isle, but we don't need to be anymore. It'll be okay." I say it all but of course there's no sound and he doesn't hear. Just stumbles onwards pleading to the empty air.

I hear a low snicker and turn to see one of Hughes' flatfoots taking photos. That brings everything back into sharp focus. My plans are not the only ones in play here. Danny might be facing life in prison, and bellowing "I'm sorry" to no-one in an empty marsh is the kind of thing to suggest remorse and therefore guilt to a jury. Contrition mixes with anger. I head directly for the bridge.

I may be able to stay away from my body for hours more, but this time it's already been too long.

I see Mrs. Canning sitting by me when I return. She looks furious. I do the usual uncontrollable gasp of reunion and my eyes open. Instantly she's on the radio to Eric.

"She's back. Raise the bridge," she snaps. The rumbling of the motor in the wall starts in immediate response. "Keep a lookout for Danny and take the boat round to get him when he appears. Call him now to say we've got her."

She grabs my arm and hauls me upright. I don't want to stand yet. My body is always dazed and weak after I've been away from it. By the time I realise where she's taking me it's too late and my muscles won't work fast enough to fight or flee. She pushes me inside and slams the door shut. I hammer on it uselessly.

"I'm okay," I moan. "It's alright because I'm okay now."

There's no reply, and nor does sound penetrate here. I call it the cell. They had it made when I was fifteen and the situation got nightmarish on a daily basis. It's a ten foot by ten foot windowless room, and its four walls, the floor, the ceiling and the door are all lined with lead, through which my ghost cannot pass.

I go to the bed and sit. Anger is still bubbling away in me but I damp it down. There's no hurry. Actually it's better if Danny takes the time to calm down before we talk.

There's plenty of time. There's all the time in the world now.

It's a full two hours before Danny comes in. He shuts the door behind him even though he can see I'm awake and watching him. I'm expecting him to launch into a rant.

"The writer. Thomas. Can he go out of his body like you?" he demands, and suddenly ice-cold fear is throttling me.

"What?"

"Can the writer go out of his body? He's lying on his bed and we can't wake him. It's the exact way you do."

Did he follow me out? I glance up at the wall clock and do rapid sums. If so it's been close on four hours since I lowered the bridge. That's longer than he can survive. Please, please let him just be spying somewhere on the island!

"When was he last awake?" I gasp.

"I'm asking the questions," Danny says. I'm about to fly off the handle at him and tell him to lose the stupid hard-man act, but the newly-mature part of me realises there's not time.

"Yes, Thomas is a ghost too. I think he's trapped outside the drawbridge. We have to hurry."

"You think I'm falling for that? You're staying right here and the drawbridge stays up."

There have been plenty of times I've hit him for much less than that. His right eye has poor peripheral vision and landing a good slap always gives me catlike satisfaction. But again there's no time. I lean forward and take his hand.

"For how long does the drawbridge stay up Danny? Until when? I finally saw it today. I'm not Bella, nor Laoise. I can trust myself now. You can trust me too."

His Adam's apple bobs. He seems at a loss for words.

"Danny you've protected me like your own flesh and blood, but what's the point of that if never to deliver me to a place of freedom?"

He bows his head. I've imagined this moment countless times. What I never guessed was that I might be barely engaged with it. My fear for Thomas is all I can think about.

"Danny we have to lower the drawbridge right now and go

and find him. Every second counts." I think I've got through to him, so I risk standing and walking towards the door. He follows, and as we run down the two flights of stairs I try to explain my fear to him, terrifying myself further as I do.

"As you know, the longer a ghost is out of their body the slower they get. I think eventually you just stay in one place, and if you leave it too long you simply dissolve away. If he followed me he's been away for between two and four hours, and from what I've seen he's not used to doing much more than one. I'm the only one who can see him so I need to go as a ghost to look. If I find him I'll need both parts of myself to direct you, and if he's unresponsive we'll need to take his flesh to his ghost. You and Eric get Thomas' body and put it next to mine in the back of the Range Rover."

"Next to yours?"

"Yes. I need to go right now. Hurry! Drive to the land end of the bridge and wait there for me to wake up."

Say what you like about Danny but he's instant in a crisis. He's moving fast and snapping commands at Eric even as I lie down across the back seat of the car and will myself out of my body. Need speeds me and in less than a minute I'm flying back over the already-lowered bridge.

Oh Thomas, where are you? Where are you?

Please don't be gone. You can't be gone. I'd...

34.

Darkness begins to grow not long after I arrive in the marshes. For a while I wander without direction. Then I decide to be logical and return to the end of the bridge.

Where would I go on a first escape from Penitent's Isle? Stretching north is only marshland. West is a vast landfill site that turns the air here malodorous when the wind blows that way. No, her balcony view looks east towards Purfleet, and maybe to her that's a place of intrigue and excitement and where she would head. So I set off on the path to it. I can feel the sadness forming around my edges, and it's a sand timer. She went out before I did, so whatever I'm feeling she is more than feeling, and if I have to hurry for my own sake then the need is greater for hers.

And yet I see nothing and I sense nothing. As I draw near the rows of brown, ambitionless housing that blights all south England I become convinced she has not passed this way, so I turn around and retrace my steps.

It's as I once again stand on the shore looking at Danny's island that I hear a motor whirr. Suddenly the drawbridge chains go taught and it begins to rise. I rush to the pier as fast as I'm able, but by the time I reach the edge the gap is insurmountable. Grey water slops around the pillars. I'm trapped away from my body, already weakened, and growing more and more fearful by the second.

After drifting in anxious, futile circles I go to the car park where Hughes' men are stationed. I can think of nothing else to try. Cathy can manipulate objects. Maybe I can work out the trick. Will they have a pen and paper? Perhaps I could write. I'm a writer. Surely it would be a natural thing? Island - stop - Quick - stop - Proof of murder - stop - Captive woman.

One policeman snoozes. The other chews gum. They have a biro and a crossword they seem to be stuck on. Nine down and six across are obvious, but I cannot produce any physical effect. I try my insubstantial hand at the radio and the car's controls in vain. I touch the chewer's flesh, which is a horrible, sticky sensation, and why I'm careful never to go too near the living. He sneezes, which wakes his colleague.

"Alwight. Doze off did I?"

"Yeah."

"Anything 'appnin'?"

"Nah. Decker went back inside on the boat. Losin' 'is marbles I reckon."

"You 'ungry?"

"Yeah, gettin' peckish. Fancy some pizza?"

"Sounds nice, yeah."

In despair I drift away and back towards the island. I'm desperately weak now and growing more sluggish by the second. The drawbridge is still up. If they've got her back it won't be going down again.

Oh Cathy, my kindred. To have come so close to something that might have been so incredible. And now I'll never know. I have no dying breath so cannot even speak it aloud; I may not yet know you, but I know I love you.

I sink to the ground and can no longer move. I have lost all will and this world is a grey and barren place. As it begins to fade from my sight I embrace its passing. Like a bad novel I've gone too far into to put aside, the end can't come soon enough. Only the regret I will never see Cathy again endures. It's the single thread preventing me from vanishing into the abyss, and even that thread grows thinner and thinner now.

35.

As soon as I cross the drawbridge I'm scanning the shore. Glancing back at the island I see the car headlights come through the gate, bringing our two bodies. I just need to know where to direct them.

If he's still here.

If what's in that car is still anything more than a corpse.

For a second the gulf that took my mother yawns, but I grip my newfound sanity and it holds.

Then I spot him, but so faint. He lies beside the path a short way west of the bridge. I fly to him but he shows no sign of awareness and doesn't move. He barely retains his own form.

"No!" I shriek silently. "No! Stay with me Thomas."

But I'm losing him. This is the end of a ghost I'm witnessing. Desperately I do the only thing I can think of and merge myself with his form, trying to supply him with the shape and strength to hold himself together.

Then I see him! Oh how I see him! I've watched enough physical intimacy between people on late-night TV; it looks fun but this is something wholly other. I read his story. I can follow the threads of his being through the human tapestry. He is at its edge. Somehow as woven apart as I am despite his very different circumstances. I desire nothing more than that our fabric stays intertwined from this moment forth. I cannot be without him.

And then I feel him watching. He's still weak as a kitten, but I know that every last thing I feel he feels too.

"Can you hold on just one minute more?" I ask the practical question forgetting speech doesn't work for ghosts.

"Yes," he replies inside me.

I don't think. I can't think yet. I part excruciatingly from him and hasten to where Danny waits with the car engine running. Eric sits beside him and Mrs. Canning is next to my body in the back. I return to myself and push through the fog of waking.

"Just up the road," I gasp. "Where those two bushes are. Hurry."

Danny drives and I have the door open before he's even fully stopped. Stumbling over I call back, "Bring him here." Danny and Eric haul Thomas' lanky frame from the boot and carry it over. I've remembered the exact place his ghost lies. They set the body down there and we all stand back and wait.

Suddenly he inhales, a tearing sound. I gasp and sink to the ground to hold him.

"You're back my love, you're back. Breathe. Hold on."

And gradually he finds a rhythm and I feel his chest loosen. I'm so focused that I don't even hear the car pull up.

"Alwight, 'old it right there! Step back. 'ands in the air, all of you." The copper has his gun out. He has a greasy tomato stain down the front of his shirt.

"Thomas? Can you 'ear me Thomas? What 'appened? Are you okay? What they done to you?" Second Cop is a twenty questions fan.

Thomas sits up and everyone watches him, but the next voice to speak is Mrs. Canning's.

"Under what powers are you asking these questions?"

"Er, Criminal Justice and Public Order Act, innit," states Copper Two with a jowl-wobbling nod.

"Of 1994? Interesting choice," replies Mrs. Canning. "Risky. Are you sure about that?"

"Listen," he snarls back. "Look at 'im. What 'appened son?"

"Section 50 of the Police Reform Act 2002," blurts Copper One smugly.

"Deary, deary me." Mrs. Canning's smile is pure rictus.

"Leave it out will you lady," barks Copper Two.

I shut the bickering out because this is all going to come down to what Thomas says next. They know who he is. None of the four of us used his name in their hearing, and yet they call him by it. My reading is that Hughes got to him. Whether that happened before Thomas took the job here or after doesn't really matter. If he goes with them his cover's blown but he's safe. If he comes with us back to Penitent's Isle he's taking a colossal risk.

I want him to take that risk.

"Please," I whisper, looking into his eyes.

Flatfoot Two gives me an irritated glance but doesn't understand what he's objecting to.

"Thank you for your concern, officers," Thomas says after what seems an age. "But I'm fine. I'll be returning to the island now."

"Not bloody likely! They got you under duress or somefink? What's goin' on?"

"As the lady already suggested to you, I'm not legally required to answer that. I'm not under duress and everything's fine."

"Nuh-uh," Copper One is still waving his gun around. "This is all too bleedin' fishy. You're coming back to the station with us Thomas."

"No I'm not."

"I say you are."

Thomas' eyes narrow and for a glorious second I think he's going to punch the copper's lights out.

"Tell Hughes that if he wants me to spy for him he should avoid sending henchmen moronic enough to call me by name. I'm returning to the island with these people. Now fuck off."

And, grudgingly, they do. Or at least they stand there not interfering as the five of us get into the car.

"Seatbelts on," says Mrs. Canning. "We have thirty yards of public road to the bridge. Don't give them a reason."

Apart from that no-one speaks until we're back inside the gate. Then Danny turns and his eyes are awful.

"Cathy, I don't want you listening in on this. You go to the lead room for now."

I want to object and demand, but this is the Danny that built an East End empire. He's hard as rock and nothing I say will deflect him. I cast one helpless look at Thomas and then get out with Eric and Mrs. Canning. She walks silently alongside me and we go into the house, up the stairs, through the small bedroom where the wardrobe door has been left open, up to the second floor, and into the cell. Once I'm inside she gently shuts the door.

Now I can only wait, in my body and in blind hope.

36.

He shuts the car door and we walk into the main house and the study. I'm numb, a little from my brush with death but mostly from Cathy's merging with me. I would never have believed any form of connection could come close to what I felt.

That was why the sensible option of getting clear with Hughes' two men was never even a possibility. Nothing holds meaning for me without her anymore. Even answers about my father's death come nowhere close. The sadness would come within or without my body and I wouldn't endure. Saving my skin tonight would have meant killing my soul.

But I want more than ever to live. And that means I have to think fast. Danny's face contains all the indecision and compassion of a crocodile's.

"Interesting decision Thomas," he says. "I don't understand what you're playin' at. Let's fix that."

"My truth for yours," I reply.

"Do you think you're in a position to be making demands? Hughes set this whole thing up and you're his mole."

"No. He found out I was coming here and tried to lean on me. I've given him nothing to date. I contacted you about this job because the idiot Americans finally twigged that Shinelle Grimes is an educated middle-class woman masquerading as socially-deprived. As I have previous in that area I lost my gig writing Frank Geyser stories for her and the agency dumped me. Your autobiography was the only job available. Hughes wasn't involved. It was only ever about making my mortgage payments."

Danny grins nastily. "Nice to see my ghost values my life story."

"I might if you gave me enough of one. So how about I tell you everything I know about the Hughes and Norris murders and you cough up your side?"

"You still think I killed them, don't you? I didn't."

"Then I don't know why you won't give me details that show that. Hughes thinks you only want an autobiography to bias the jury when he puts you on trial again. I believe he's right."

"That's more or less why Mrs. Canning wants it. I have other reasons."

"Such as?"

"Not likely. But I'll accept about Hughes and Norris. So go on then. What makes you so bloody sure I'm a murderer?"

"You know I can leave my body. I can also read anything written on any piece of paper even inside a closed book."

"Useful trick in your line of work. Was it you gave Cathy the bridge code?"

"Yes. I've also seen your blackmail files upstairs. There are some high-up hypocrites in there."

"Okay, you've made your point. So?"

"When I was working with Sid I knew he was palming me off with amusing tales and characters more than real content. The raconteur side was adequate for the publisher, but I was curious so I went wandering."

Danny can't help himself. He leans forwards. Sid's secrets: is this why he wanted me and only me to write his autobiography?

"You know the risk of police raids well enough, and that Sid's no fool. There was nothing written down about the murders, but I found a receipt for the watch you gave Mrs.

Canning and I assume Sid gave you. Sid ordered it the morning after Hughes and Norris were killed, and it says 'World's Best Cleaner' on the back. It's hardly subtle."

Danny looks oddly disappointed. "That watch could go into the Thames right now. The jeweller burned down in '82, and without their records there's no more evidence."

"I know. I actually believe you when you say you didn't kill them. That's why I've given you the only thing I could have told Hughes. The grenade pin detail came from him, by the way, not Sid. And Hughes says they have a DNA match for you from it. That's going to be their justification for a retrial, I guess."

"I did drop the grenade into that car."

I blink. "But you keep saying you didn't kill them...?"

"I didn't. They were already dead. I just cleaned things up, didn't I? Like the fucking watch says."

It's all I can do not to exclaim "Aha!" There's no sensation of the stairs bookshelf listening today, and I wonder if Cathy knows this already? Concern for her comes piling into my mind and it's a struggle to recentre myself in the study where Danny is finally telling me the truth, the whole truth and nothing but the truth.

"Sid knew full well Norris was passing information to the boys in blue. He was feeding him a nice crock of shit to screw up half of their ongoing investigations. He didn't want to kill him."

"Sid killed Norris?"

"'E 'ad to. Took half a day making it painful. I'd 'ave made it much worse."

Danny's face is perhaps the most frightening thing I've ever seen in my life. Finally he closes his eyes in pain. "Terry Norris raped Sid's daughter."

"Bella?"

It's a stupid thing to say, but he replies simply, "Yes."

I'm doing maths: summer 1975 to March the 15th 1976 equals nine months. "So Cathy...?" It explains what's in that manilla envelope.

"Yes. But Bella and Cathy aren't part of today's deal Thomas."

I nod in understanding.

"I got the call mid-afternoon. The warehouse was like an abattoir. Blood everywhere. I must have looked like I wanted to run because Sid told me straight out why 'e'd done it. I thought I'd kept 'ow I felt about Bella secret, but I'd been fooling no-one. So Sid starts laying out his whole plan. 'E'll be the cops' main target so 'e'll be elsewhere with a rock-solid alibi. Blowing up the bodies will disguise the time of death. I pick up on the word bodies and 'e says yes, two of them. If only Norris dies the investigation will lead back to what happened to Bella because it was in a cinema and there were witnesses saw the two of them go in together. 'We don't want that for her do we Danny? For her reputation?' 'e says. I shake my head and he nods. 'So the slimy shit's been flogging information to the rozzers an' 'e and his contact are due to meet tomorrow. If it looks like the two of them get the chop there and then no-one's going to come poking around Bella, right? It'll go down as a grass getting his dues, nothin' more.'"

"So Brian Hughes wasn't dead at this point?"

"No. 'E was staying in a local 'otel as part of 'is cover as a building inspector. Sid collected from the place and arranged the staff roster so the right people were there to make a fake breakfast order and room service record for the next morning. This nasty piece of work called Larry the Lizard done Hughes with a garotte that night. It would 'ave been clean and quick."

I really don't want to dwell on this so scrabble for a way to move the conversation on. "But there was a photo of Norris at a poker game the evening before the explosion. You were in it in fact. Hughes used it in court to say you were close to Terry and helped set him up.”

“Our forger made that. Old guy who’d worked for the MoD doing German IDs in the war. ’E was good. It was all just to distract from Bella. Only Hangman-bloody-Hughes got the idea to use it with a fake witness testimony placing me with Norris that day and up to an hour before the recorded time of death. That’s what got me the six months for perverting the course of justice.”

And while he was inside and couldn’t protect her Bella left her body and never returned, and Sid could never forgive Danny for that failure. I want to tell him it wasn’t his fault, but I think he might kill me on the spot if I tried. Fortunately he resumes his story.

“We did a switch to get Brian Hughes’ car, then...”

“A switch?” If I want the story I need the details.

“Truck drives up and blocks the view of Hughes’ car from the ’otel. Someone drives in an identical model and colour and parks in the same space right after I get out the truck and use Hughes’ key to drive ’is away. Truck moves off with the other driver in, and there’s one brown car, same as before. You’d ’ave to be very unlucky for anyone to notice the difference.”

“Clever.”

“Thorough. Sid was always that. Hughes’ body goes out in a laundry van and then we load ’im and what was left of Norris into the back seat. At the time their meeting’s arranged I drive it to the location, get out, post a long-fuse grenade in through the window, and walk away.”

“Leaving the pin behind?”

“Seems so. I honestly don’t remember. By the way, apart from me and you only Mrs. Canning knows any of this. And Cathy too, some of it anyway.”

"Thank you, Danny." There's a lengthy pause. "So should we talk about Cathy?"

"No. Next I'm going to talk with Cathy about you. When I'm done I'll let you know and then it's whatever comes next. Until then Mrs. Canning will sit with you to make sure you don't close your eyes and go eavesdropping. Try it and you won't 'ave a living body to return to."

I take no umbrage at this. In fact I respect it.

37.

Previous times when I've been locked in here, I've been either waiting out of body to flit through when the door opens or I've been red hot and ready to rage. Today I'm controlled.

Danny seems both relieved and curious. "Shall we go to the day room instead?"

I nod and follow him. I wonder if Thomas is here listening, and that sets off a whirl of everything. "If you hurt him," I say, "my retribution will be total."

He looks at me with an unusual kind of wistfulness. "I already know that Cathy. Don't worry. What we need to discuss is what happens next."

I raise a quizzical eyebrow.

"That DNA on the grenade pin story...how much of my interviews with Thomas did you listen in on?"

"Every word."

He shakes his head, smiling. "It's from Hughes, not Sid. He told it to Thomas to convince him I was a killer. That new evidence will get Hughes his retrial, and I'm going to be put away for life."

Tears suddenly run down my cheeks. "But surely if you tell them what really happened...?"

"Brian Hughes was a copper. If The Met gets a chance to

settle this score they'll take it. And whilst Terry Norris deserved to die, Hughes didn't. Revenge is fair enough."

"But you didn't..."

"And life isn't fair. At least with what Thomas told us we get warning. Some time before they come for me."

"What if you left? What if we all left? It stinks here in The Thames. The sky is polluted orange and all the traffic never stops. You never see the stars. There's never silence. Why don't we just leave?"

Danny shakes his head again. "Islands are easily watched. Hughes has his men stationed here for exactly that reason. If he suspects I'm trying to get out of the country they'll be there to nab me at whichever port or airport and put me into custody as a flight risk. It's better just to stay put on Penitent's Isle for what time we have left."

I rise, sobbing, and go over to hold him. "Danny I'm so sorry. I've been awful to you so many time. I've cost you so much."

He pushes me back so he can look at me. "Don't ever say that Cathy. You've been the light of my life these last twenty-four years. But for you I'd have gone crazy and either killed myself or a whole load of other people."

"You loved Bella that much?"

"Yes." If it wasn't that he never cries, I think there would be a river of tears now.

"I understand. I understand because I love Thomas the same way."

"I know."

Despite the fact that I do cry and I do have tears running down my cheeks now, I start laughing. "I thought I'd have to face a thousand objections, like we just met...in fact we've never met in physical form apart from in the car earlier. I thought you'd say I was being a romantic idiot. All that."

"Cathy you're twenty-eight in March. I'm pushing sixty. Mrs. Canning and Eric should both be retired. Conventional solutions haven't worked and our situation here has gone on far too long. Add to that they could come for me any day and, well. Also I saw it in your face when you asked me to help save him. It took me less than a single second to fall in love with Bella, and I've never stopped."

I'm reeling slightly, a mix of anticipation and nerves. "So what does happen next?"

"I'm not the one to answer that. It's time I bow out and you make all your own choices. What do you want Cathy?"

"I want Thomas."

"And beyond that?"

"I have no idea. We'll work it out together." Suddenly there's a horrible new doubt. "Assuming he wants me of course."

Danny suddenly convulses. For second I think he's having some sort of seizure, but then I see it's laughter and it's completely taken him over. "Oh you've no worries on that score," he gets out before pausing to suck in air. "I've told you often enough..." he thumps the chair arm trying and failing to get control, "...how alike to your mother you are. Well when he so much as hears your name he looks exactly the way I must have when I first saw her..." he finally manages to breathe, "...the poor bastard."

38.

Since all secrets are out and time is really dragging, I ask Mrs. Canning, "So how does a barrister end up cooking and cleaning?"

She shows no sign of having heard me, but after a minute or more's silence she says, "I prefer it. The whole courts system is a smug, snobbish game that I got sick of. See no evil, hear no evil, speak no evil is all very well, but neither the police nor most felons are particularly clever. I always knew what the truth was, and justice happens a lot less often than you'd hope. A good meal from a scrubbed-clean kitchen, on the other hand, is reliably satisfying."

I nod at an excellent answer, and conversation dies again.

After an aeon her radio goes, and she stands. I make to get up too, but she looks at me and shakes her head.

Danny appears at the door. "Come on Elsie," he says to Mrs. Canning. "The situation's as bad as we feared. Let's finish the planning in your office and leave these two to it."

They go, and at long last I'm here with both halves of Cathy, who walks in and stands near the window, looking at me.

Words have always ordered themselves at my command, but I can't start. Hi, hello, nice to meet you: none work. I can muster only silence, such is the weight of everything.

Now she comes over. I see her hands are trembling, and notice mine are too. The books save us. "I couldn't live outside these walls, so Danny would bring me these," she says, caressing the spines. "They've been my windows onto the world."

We stand closer, gazing at the lines of titles chosen with such care by the greatest writers of recent centuries.

"You might be a bit skewed towards the nineteenth century," I venture. "I'm afraid it's all a bit more banal and instant these days."

"I know that. I do have a TV."

"Thank you for saving my life." My breath shudders saying it.

"Do I get to keep part of it as a reward?"

"Gladly. That connection..."

"Yes..."

"I don't think I can be apart from you."

"Nor I you." She reaches up to wrap her arms around my neck, pulling my face to hers so our lips can meet. I dissolve into the kiss. It's the polar opposite of the sadness.

"You're very tall," she notes when we finally draw apart to gaze at each other again.

"Yes. I find public transport awkward."

"Are we crazy Thomas? Can love really work this way?"

I gesture towards the rows of novels. "These claim so. And millions read them avidly."

"And your heart?"

"Never knew what it was doing or where it was going until I came to Penitent's Isle."

"How frustrating was it for you to have to talk like we did?"

"It was maddening! It made me realise what a part of me words are."

She nods. "Why don't you write books under your own name?"

I exhale. "I did try. I think perhaps I've spent too long fitting myself to others' expectations. I can mimic a voice and winkle out someone else's story, but I'm not sure my own have ever found fertile soil to grow in."

"That's so English."

"Isn't it."

"I would never let someone else put their name on my books."

The second floor day room comes back into my mind. In the corner near the balcony with its view east there was a desk with a typewriter and reams of paper. "Do you write?" I ask.

She shrugs. "I don't know if you could call them novels."

"Now who's being English!"

She laughs and I pull her to me and kiss her again. And again, and again. I've experienced physical closeness before but it's been utterly superficial by comparison.

"Ohh this!" she says, "I wonder how long we get?"

"A lifetime," I reply.

"But how long is that?"

I lean back and look down to study her.

"I'm twenty-eight soon. My mother and grandmother were ghosts and neither made it past their mid-twenties. You're...?"

"Thirty," I say quietly. Puzzle pieces are slotting together, but horribly. "You think what we are is genetic? And that our species is short-lived."

She nods. "Who was it on your side?"

"My dad," I realise through a sudden wave of sadness. "I never really knew him. He was twenty-nine. I was six." Questions I suppose I've always had about him, and how and why he left us, now get answers. Head-spinning answers I understand too intimately. Emotions remain dammed up inside me, but, strangely, their easing has already begun. If that sorrow will always be part of my fabric, there's a small, bereft boy's anger that can perhaps start to be unpicked from it.

And for the here and now, that's three murders Danny's been cleared of today.

Cathy, who's been quietly watching, reaches up to hold me and plants another kiss on my lips. "But my new theory is there's a medicine. Us. I know how we end, and it's been seeming closer of late. But now it's never felt further away."

"It's not that our kind can't go on, it's just that we can't do it alone?" I believe she's right. I hope she's right.

"Either way I suggest we try the hell out of it."

As I nod agreement she pulls me tightly to her and winds herself against me. I'm intoxicated and the world is filled with light and hope and I never want this moment in the sudden sun to end.

Time doesn't stop though, and after a while context begins

to grow impatient and make its presence felt.

"I don't know what happens next," I murmur at last.

"Me neither. Only that we are together for as long as."

"Yes."

"Should I get Danny? He's blessed...this, by the way."

I'd surmised as much, not being at the bottom of the Thames and so on, but I'm still glad to hear it. "I suppose so, but before you do I have to ask if he's keeping you captive here?"

She looks at me thoughtfully. "Back story?"

"It does aid understanding."

She nods and gestures me to the sofa, sitting down next to me and taking my hand.

"I've heard all your conversations with Danny so I won't repeat what you already know. I'm Bella's daughter, but not his. My biological father was Terry Norris."

She's looking at me presumably expecting shock. "Ah," she says when I don't show it. "He told you that earlier when I was upstairs?"

"Yes. And the truth about what happened to Brian Hughes and Norr...your father."

"I don't think of him that way. If I have a father it's Danny. And he's done all he's done even though I was a living reminder of the woman he adored and lost. And of what was done to her and by whom."

It's torture worthy of classical literature. To say anything would only sound glib.

"Even before Terry Norris raped Bella she wanted free of the world. I think she loved Danny in a grateful sort of way, but it was half-hearted. I don't believe she had the capacity for anything else, especially afterwards. Not for me either. I don't even remember her. Danny's always struggled to speak about it, but Mrs. Canning told me. She blamed herself for not getting him acquitted on the perverting the course of justice charge. Danny blamed himself for not being there when Bella departed. Sid blamed everyone else, even as he walked free."

"Sid has no idea you exist, does he? Never having grandchildren was a source of real sadness to him."

She flares up. "That's a bit bloody rich. He was a terrible, controlling, cheating insensitive brute of a husband. He should have married a waxwork doll if that was what he wanted. Not a starry-eyed teenager straight off a farm in Ireland just because she was beautiful and sang like an angel. From what Mrs. Canning says he barely noticed Bella until she started maturing and other men began eyeing her. Then he turned into some hideous mixture of doting and dictator. It's little wonder her life went as it did."

"I'm not sure he knew any better," I venture quietly. "His life genuinely was as hard as the cliches. I'm not sure he's ever experienced trust or love."

She considers me. "It's so odd that you know my grandfather far better than I do or even Danny does. And to answer your question, no, as far I know, and for all the reasons I've just given, he has no idea about me. In fact this was something we badly wanted you to confirm. It's why I insisted Danny hire the same writer who did Sid's autobiography."

"It was your idea for him to hire me?"

"Yes. If I've been in some ways a captive here sometimes, it hasn't been in the powerless and uninformed sense. In my clear-headed moments I asked Danny to do all that he did in the times I just wanted to dissolve away."

Now worry finds a foothold on her face. "But I do believe something fundamental has changed Thomas. I don't believe you're taking on a madwoman."

"I don't care."

"Still," she says with a teasing smile. "Life's always more

pleasant with a bit less insanity, isn't it?"

"I suppose," I concur. "Anyway you haven't heard the dreadful details of my life yet."

"Are they very psychotic?"

"No. My fear is you'll be bored to tears."

We laugh, we kiss again several times, and then she goes off to fetch Danny and I miss her already.

Oh Dad, I wish you could have experienced what I'm feeling now in your too-soon-over life. It's the elixir.

39.

Danny and Mrs. Canning look up when I knock on her apartment door. Her face is etched with concern. His is resigned.

"There's been another development," Mrs. Canning says. "It's not good news."

"All the more reason to go to the study and involve Thomas then." I reply.

Mrs. Canning looks surprised, but Danny nods agreement.

"Eric too?" she asks.

"Of course," replies Danny.

The groundsman is radioed in from the cold, and when he arrives we all file off down the hall.

Thomas is perusing the bookshelf when we enter, and it's all I can do not to grab him and pull him into me. I know this should be a delicate and sombre moment, but life-loving verve has sprung up in me and simply can't be plugged. He nods politely and we all go over and sit round the coffee table. I take his hand. Danny looks pleased if anything. Eric studies his boots. Mrs. Canning doesn't react.

"It's getting very late," she says. "There's a little to tell, and then why don't I go and make us all some supper?"

I don't think anyone has any appetite, but we all nod at the common sense of it.

She continues, "It seems our excursion earlier has pushed things into motion. As you know we've got the prosecutor's secretary's office bugged, and she took a call right at the end of the working day requesting an urgent meeting tomorrow. From what I could hear the police want a formal motion for retrial and to interview Danny under oath and compel him to provide a DNA sample. Hughes is making his move."

Thomas gives a peculiar smile during that, and I tug his hand and look questioningly at him. "What?"

He shrugs. "It's irrelevant now and I don't hold any grudge, but finding out you'd bugged my flat almost pushed me into helping Hughes."

"We didn't bug your flat," says Danny, frowning.

"The police play dirty Thomas," Mrs. Canning states. "I'm surprised you haven't grasped that by now. Clever trick to make you think we had though."

"Oh," he says simply, and squeezes my hand back by way of apology.

Danny moves on. "Chances are they'll try to remand me in custody. We could be talking only days."

Eric looks up gaping, hand juddering to his mouth.

"And then what?" Thomas asks. "Hughes said the DNA technology wasn't verified yet. He didn't seem sure of his case or his witnesses either. They can't keep you locked up indefinitely in those circumstances can they? Or am I being naïve," he adds when the pairs of eyes looking at him narrow.

"The rules for the East End have always been different," Danny says. "Once they have me behind bars the only way I expect to leave prison again is in a coffin."

"So," Mrs. Canning takes over, "In the time left it makes sense to get affairs in order. First, we can assume they'll manage to obtain a search warrant. Danny, is there a plan for everything we wouldn't want them to find?"

"All the documents of value are computerised, right? Maureen will see USB drives get to where they're needed. The hard copies go up in flames...sorry, I expect you don't want to know the actual details Mrs. C.."

"It'd be appreciated."

"Then there's just a few things for Eric to drop off the boat and that should be the place clean enough. The cash here gets split as needed. There'll be more from the club as and when. You know you'll all be looked after for life, right? And you can treat this place as home as long as you want."

"There are likely to be civil cases for damages and also state confiscation of criminally-acquired assets," Mrs. Canning corrects. "I think it's better we don't rely on the status quo."

Everyone's faces are sinking and so is my heart as we talk about the people left behind and what they'll do. This is my family, and it's about to be violently broken apart.

"Or..." says Thomas, making all gazes swivel to him.

He takes a deep breath. "We bring the true story out. I admit it's a stretch, but arguably what Danny did only amounted to perversion of the course of justice, and he's already been convicted and jailed for that so double jeopardy could still apply. Would Hughes do a deal for just Sid?"

Danny smiles as if humouring a child. "The DNA match is with me. The only way Sid ends up in court here is if he confesses."

"I think he might."

Eric's face has creased into a confused frown.

"Get real Thomas," snaps Danny. "That self-interested old bastard wouldn't lift a finger to help me, let alone chuck his life away on a murder charge."

"He might if his granddaughter asked him. You see I think

he's dying."

Mrs. Canning's mouth has fallen open and none of the other two are doing much better. I, on the other hand, feel like there's a fire been lit in me. I have faith in my pirate king.

"Can you explain that?" asks Danny cautiously.

"He was buying his place in Spain whilst I was interviewing him for 'As Nails'. He was also having secret treatment for lung cancer. One day near the end he left a message cancelling our session, but I didn't get it and turned up at his house as originally planned. It was a wet, miserable morning and although he was in pyjamas and looked shattered he let me in and offered me tea. As we drank it he told me that one day soon he would have had all he could take of the chemotherapy and would jack it in and go off to Spain to try and find peace while he could. He moved there fourteen months ago. I don't know his exact prognosis, but I assume he must be in the terminal stages."

Danny shakes his head. "No. They've got good hospitals out there on the Costas. He'll have changed his mind and gone over for more treatment. He wouldn't just give up like that. Not Sid."

"His place isn't on the Costas. It's up in the remote northwest on the Atlantic coast. He showed me photos and talked about how it was away from everyone and everything and all there was was the crash of the waves and the wind in the trees. It's not a place you'd go for specialist medical services."

I lean forward. "Do we lose anything by trying? Thomas and I aren't wanted so we're free to travel. We could be there tomorrow. His ghostwriter and a woman with his darling Bella's face? He's not going to turn us away. If we get inside, tell him who I am and ask and then he says no, we're no worse off, are we?"

Mrs. Canning and Eric sit frozen, waiting for Danny's reply.

"Okay," he says finally. "I don't think you've a hope in hell, but if your choice is to try then okay."

I take Thomas' hand, seeking strength and finding it willingly given. He nods in answer to my glance. "It is our choice," I say.

40.

It all feels rather like the end of Trinity term. Eric is the first to leave, pleading something that needs doing to the slugs. Mrs. Canning and Danny stand and mention housekeeping to take care of. And then it's just Cathy and I. She rises and looks at me, and I follow her without a word being spoken.

We go out and to the small gate. She pulls out a key and opens it and we walk out onto the grass. It's far into nighttime now but orange haze fills the air and a passing ship with thudding diesel engines blazes floodlights to add a sharp white hue to the murk. It's easy to see the apple tree is bare of the last of its leaves. She's wearing only jeans and a thin jumper, and hugs herself against the November cold.

"Are you okay?" I venture, putting an arm around her.

"Yes. Just a little nervous."

"Of?"

"Everything."

"I get that. What's top of the list? Flying?"

"No, sex. Don't get me wrong, I really want to, but I've never done it before. Obviously."

My eyebrows jump for my hairline. "There's absolutely no rush with that. I should mention I find you breathtakingly attractive."

She smiles at that. "I presume you're experienced? It's good one of us is."

"A little, but what we have is a first for me. When you

merged your ghost with mine..."

"It wasn't a violation, was it Thomas? It was all I could think of to do. You were disappearing and I had to keep you here."

"You saved my life. Also it was the most incredible experience of all my days on Earth. It's why I came back to Penitent's Isle rather than play safe and go with the police. Being apart from you just wasn't an option after that."

"I know! But now everything's going to change. I must have walked this boring little path ten thousand times wishing to be elsewhere...but suddenly elsewhere's looming very large."

"Yes." I hug her tight. She's lithe and alive and I desire her beyond words. She's also shivering. "Should we go in?" I ask.

"Soon. I've been missing my walks out here lately."

"Because of me?"

"Because of you. Tell me, does the whole world smell like this?"

"No. Literally almost everywhere else smells much better."

She smiles. "Then I can't wait to explore it."

A thought suddenly occurs to me. "Do you have a passport? I think I saw your birth certificate and it had been left blank."

"Yes, I have a passport. Danny can get anything and he's very thorough. Do you want to hear something amusing? It's Irish, courtesy of my grandma."

I laugh into the East London mist. "Really? I'm surprised Danny lets you in the house."

"He says he only hates the ones who plant bombs."

"That's a fair point. Actually a lot of his points are fair when you consider them."

She nods and pulls even tighter into my side. "He's a good man. I don't want him to go to prison."

I can feel the sobs starting where she's pressed against me. "Let's go and get some sleep. We've got a busy day tomorrow. I do think we stand a chance you know."

"I hope so. Come upstairs with me while I get something to sleep in. Then I prefer we go to the cottage. The second floor isn't my home anymore."

And an hour later I'm lying in bed and the ghost from my dreams who turned my world on its head is bodily-warm against me.

She breathes deep sleeping breaths, warm wonderful life into my desiccated soul.

41.

"Are you awake?" I whisper.

"Never more so." He sounds alert.

"I wouldn't have imagined you as a morning person."

"I'm not really. By choice I get up for the last few hours of the night to write, then go back to bed until eleven."

"Is that when you wrote Sid's book? In the night?"

"Mostly. You've read it then?"

"Of course. It may be the most read book in the library. Apart from Wuthering Heights, which I know back-to-front."

"That's one of my favourite novels too. Another Cathy. Er... did Danny mention anything else I've written?"

He sounds more than a little ashamed, which by all accounts is about right. "Do you mean the Frank Geyser series or I Still See The Light? Did that ever get printed by the way? I haven't read either."

"Please don't! Or at least not until we're old and grey and want to look back and laugh at life's absurdity."

"Thomas." I lever myself up onto an elbow to look at him properly. "It's time you did better than that."

"I know," he says, as the phone goes and I get up to answer it.

"Mrs Canning," I report back to him. "Our flights are

booked for noon. We should get a move on. Up and at it, writer."

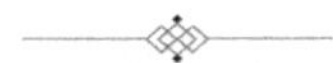

Eric and Thomas stand in the boat's cabin whilst I crouch down on the floor out of sight.

"It'll be the other two on now," mutters Eric as we pass the watchers' spot. He cleaned the glass before we left so they can get good photos of Thomas. After yesterday's shenanigans it'll take at least a little urgency out of the equation to confirm he's alive and well.

Thomas reckons Hughes will try to make contact with him at his flat. I'm curious to see this residence of my man's, but that's not on our agenda today. We're only going over the river to Crossness, where Danny has a car waiting for us. They won't be expecting that, freeing us to go unobserved directly to the airport.

Heathrow. One of the world's busiest public spaces. I feel like I should be nervous, but I'm not nervous. Should I be worried about that? Yesterday started a new lease of life, but it's currently without any parameters beyond staying near my fellow ghost.

"How are you doing?" Thomas asks, as if reading my thoughts.

"My thighs are cramping and it stinks of diesel down here," I grumble.

"Sorry."

"What are you apologising for?"

"I'm not. I'm empathising."

"Ah," I say. "I've spent too long around Danny, haven't I?"

Eric, bless him, manages a chortle at that.

A little while later he steers round a dock to a hidden mooring and we climb ashore. Thomas gets his phone returned to him and switches it on. I'm keyed up and want to get going, but he stands lost in thought and watching the boat until it's back into the main channel of the river and heading towards Penitent's Isle.

We traverse the M25 in a sea of cars that barely moves. Thomas has been busy on his phone sending a long text message, but now he takes my hand.

"What's the bigger risk, claustrophobia or agoraphobia?" he asks gently.

"I'm okay. I'm more worried about meeting Sid."

He nods at that. For all his surety yesterday I don't think he has an actual plan.

"And it's not like I've never travelled before," I continue. "I tried school twice and university once. We took a few holidays too. Yacht's nicest. Danny was always relaxed on those trips because there was water to keep me from roaming if the blackness took me."

Thomas twists more towards me. "Was it really that bad? And do you really feel cured just like that?" He snaps his long fingers.

"It was bad only in episodes, but I never knew when they would strike and they came on so suddenly. In mere moments it would be like all the colour drained from the world and it became an awful place. I just wanted to leave, and I knew I could so very easily."

"I understand," he ventures. "I call it the sadness, but for me it's something that's only quite mild when I'm whole. However it starts up as soon as I exit my body, and builds and builds the longer away in time and distance I am from it. How long was it from when you lowered the bridge to when you found my ghost?"

"Four hours, give or take."

"I was beyond my limit you know. I'd let go and everything had faded away. Then you were there and I fought and fought to return. If you hadn't given me your form to fit to I doubt I'd have managed."

"Then you never go that close again." I'm shocked at the depth of my vehemence, and take a breath to calm myself. "Is that all that's beyond, empty grey?"

"It's all I could perceive. You know that saying about the whole being greater than the sum of its parts? I believe our spirits are the difference in the equation. Letting go would simply be allowing a return to nothingness."

It makes sense. It makes more sense of me than anything I've heard or read before. "By strict laws of physics, conservation of matter and energy and so on, that would make our lives an aberration. Do you think nature is always hell bent on correcting that, in the same way it abhors a vacuum, and that's why we get these feelings?"

He shrugs. "Maybe. I don't know. But I've never felt physicists have all the answers. That's the beauty of literature and of life: facts can co-exist with mystery. How dull would it be to know everything?"

I reach up and draw him to me so I can kiss him. I'd keep him like this forever but we're pulling up at some sort of incredibly ugly concrete concourse where luggage-burdened people scurry in all directions like worker ants.

"No-one on Penitent's Isle was any good at this sort of conversation, you know. I love it. I want more of it. The world's not grey anymore Thomas. It's all vibrant colour."

I recall that last thought when we've been pointlessly standing in an overclose queue of restless people for quarter of an hour. The antonym for vibrant colour is Heathrow Terminal Three.

"Don't we have reserved seats?" I ask Thomas.

"Yes," he says from up where he's able to breathe slightly less foul air.

"Then why are we queueing?"

He considers this. "I don't know. It's just what one does in this situation."

"Could we stop doing it?"

"I suppose. It feels wrong though."

His former diffident self has been reasserting itself in subtle ways. I don't mind that though. I've seen enough hardness to last more than one lifetime. In fact I love more that he could be the pirate king but prefers not to be. My grandmother lived the life of a pirate king's wife - as Gilbert and Sullivan might have put it - and she lasted all of six years before taking the only way out of it available to her. I aspire to something better.

It's my first time on a plane and frankly I'd imagined something less the opposite of luxury. I feel like toothpaste. Thomas insists I take the window seat. Then he gets stuck trying to fit his long thigh bones in the inadequate leg-space of the middle seat and bashes his head on the overhead lockers when pulling himself free.

"This is why I hate sodding planes," he mutters.

A heavily-built man in sportswear appears, fights a wheeled suitcase into the compartment above, and then wedges himself into the aisle seat, the proximity of his stomach causing Thomas to snatch his hand clear of the shared armrest. He gives me a look that causes me to convulse in giggles.

"I'm glad you're enjoying this."

"I've never felt so good about being five-foot-five."

He smiles and takes my hand. "Are you ready for takeoff?"

"Bring it on!"

"There! Look!"

He's better at working out London seen from impossibly far above than I am. Although I'm busy being amazed by all the city centre's recognisable buildings in miniature form, I line myself up with where he's pointing, and in the brown snake of The Thames there it is: Penitent's Isle. My entire world for most of my life, and it's just a tiny, tiny, tiny little dot.

The blue of sky and sea is different here. Back home winter's around the corner and staying inside is attractive, but here there's a warmer light that thrills me and makes me want to be out in it. The plane's noises changed some minutes ago and my ears grew painful until they went pop. Suddenly there's a stretch of glorious white sand, rearing cliffs and then dark green forest. It's so close to my lifelong dreams of freedom that I almost shriek aloud.

The cabin crew have ceased being conscripted salespeople and are buckling themselves into seats. An announcement blares out in Spanish and then in English that's so heavily accented it might as well be another foreign tongue.

"Did you catch that?" I ask Thomas.

"We'll be landing in A Coruña in ten minutes. And some stuff about tray tables and not smoking that I won't bore you with."

"Do you speak Spanish?"

"Not well, I'm realising. Just enough to go on holiday, in the best British tradition."

Passing beneath us now are dockyards and industry like the

East End. Similar, but also very different. Around it there are steep green hills and a fjord-like opening to the Atlantic where a string of glorious beaches stretches north. "Do you know what city that is?" I ask.

"Ferrol I think. Birthplace of Franco."

"That's not what you'd want as a claim to fame."

"Indeed."

There's a loud clunk and a sudden sensation of movement. The roar gets louder and my heart pounds as sudden fear rises. We can't crash now! Not with so much that's so good ahead.

"It's just the wheels going down," Thomas soothes, his hand squeezing mine. "Sorry. I should have warned you."

"Never apologise!"

"Never apologise!" he parrots. "Sorry."

I laugh and it's all alright again.

"Bugger!"

"Why do you keep punching the door?" I ask, genuinely confused. Also quite alarmed because cars and pedestrians are coming from all angles and Thomas doesn't seem to be doing that well at the whole driving thing.

"It's where the gearstick should be. I've never driven on the continent before. I'll get the hang of it soon enough."

"Ah," I say, thinking how provincial it was of me not to have realised sooner.

Only when we join a near-empty motorway and it's all faster and much calmer do I relax and let my thoughts turn to the fact that we're speeding towards a first meeting with the maternal grandfather who doesn't know I exist.

And whose remaining few days we're going to ask for as sacrifice, albeit a just and more-than-deserved one.

And then, suddenly, there's no more motorway. Only half-built sky-bridges that glide effortlessly over the kind of winding valley we're now slogging up and down through.

"What does the map say?" shouts Thomas, the articulated lorry right on our rear bumper stressing him.

"It doesn't even have the motorway we were on on it. I think we're going through a place called Fene. Look for any turning signposted to Ortigueira."

We pass through close-packed five-storey buildings in clashing, garish colours and tile patterns. Occasionally there will be a gap, the sides of the neighbouring blocks covered in ugly corrugated roofing boards. Then suddenly we're into countryside again and there are cows and chickens and the kind of ramshackle homes that look like they belong to a colony of survivalists.

The fields are astonishingly green for late November. As we rise up out of a steep valley trees appear, and then they are the only things around us. A hundred feet tall they must be. Ramrod-straight trunks fighting each other to reach the sky. In one place they're cutting them down. It's a devastating scar on the landscape, but the smell is wonderful.

"Are they eucalyptus?" I ask.

"I've no idea," replies Thomas, who seems to have mastered driving the wrong way round and is now enjoying going fast.

"Why did Sid come here? It's completely alien."

Thomas lets the car slow to a more sedate pace. "I don't entirely know, but I think that was the point. He'd never left the East End and it seemed to be that if he did he wanted a complete change. We only talked about it briefly a couple of times, but he said anywhere on the Costa-Del-Sol would have been too much a home from home. Plus he didn't like the heat. Apparently it rains here more than anywhere else in Spain, and he said that was his favourite sort of weather."

"I still can't work it out Thomas. Do you like Sid or not?" This has been bugging me for some while.

"I'd rather not try to decide. I'm here essentially because I love you and you love Danny and want to help him. Only Sid can do that, and I feel only you can give him cause to. Secondary characters shouldn't set the tone."

I can't argue with that, however much I'd like to. "You're fond of a literary cliché as an escape route, aren't you?"

He grins. "Absolutely." He negotiates a corner and then glances at me thoughtfully. "I've a favour to ask you."

"You can have any favour you want from me. Don't you know that?"

"This is a bit different."

"Go on then."

"Tell me about these not-quite-novels you write."

More tight corners appear on the steep hill we're descending and they afford me a minute to consider how I feel about this. I've made damn sure no-one else has ever read a word I've written.

"Surely you know a writer should always show, not tell," I rejoin.

"Hoist by my own petard," he laughs. "Fair enough."

"But you can read one when we get back if you'd like."

He looks across at me for a dangerously long moment. "I'd love that."

And forget suddenly seizing life in your late twenties, forget Heathrow, forget flying, forget Spanish roads and forget Sid; this is how it feels to be terrified.

42.

I really wasn't sure how Cathy would cope with going

straight from her gilded prison to the jammed-in hellscape of international air travel. Even how she'd adapt to being with me and away from the three warders she's known all her life. But if she's experiencing any kind of turmoil she keeps it remarkably well-hid.

She seems joyous in fact. She reaches to me often for a tiny contact. I love it. I love her. Touch isn't a shock now, but that's because that amazing electricity is there in me constantly like a hundred-percent-charged battery. I feel fully alive. It shines a light on the extent to which I wasn't.

We reach Ortigueira successfully and drive through it and beyond towards the farthest north tip of Spain. Espasante turns out to be a fishing village straddling the narrow neck of a small peninsula. Only when we've found the hotel Mrs. Canning booked, checked in and walked out from the huddled streets do we really see where we are. Mountains meet ocean here. It's wild and clean and it's quite astonishingly beautiful.

The winter sun has a foreign warmth to it, but it's still sinking low towards the stunning range of hills to our west. I look at my watch and see it's approaching five.

"Are we going today?" I ask. "We don't need to if you prefer to acclimatise a bit first."

"No. We don't know when Hughes will make his move, so every hour counts. How do we get there?"

Again I'm amazed by how calm she seems and I'm tempted to double-check she's truly okay with everything, but I don't want that course set for this relationship. She says she's fine and I never wish to doubt that.

"It's a bit over half a mile to our east. How do you feel about walking it?" I'm hoping she'll say yes because I've had enough of Spanish driving for today and I still haven't stretched out properly after the flight.

She's gazing at everything around us with a kind of awe, and it occurs to me that if I find it so beautiful, how must it impress someone who's known only a view of a power station and the M25? "I would love to," she breathes. "Please let's."

So we do, along an arc of sand that the low sun reddens. We're the only ones here. There aren't even footprints from anyone or anything else except seabirds. We're alone together, our shadows long and stretching far into the pathless expanse ahead.

Splitting the beach is a small headland. Rather than chance the rocks where waves crash, we climb a goat-type track over it. At the top she stops. "I could live here. I mean really live here."

She's right. This is a place for forging connections with your soul. I understand why Sid chose it now.

We kiss. We kiss again. Frankly I want nothing more than to sink down into the sea-stunted grass and enjoy the thrilling way nature has constructed man and woman with her, but real-world time is marching too-rapidly onwards.

"That's his house over there," I say, pointing to the cliff-edge chalet at the far end of the next stretch of beach. I recognise it from the photos he showed me.

We kiss one last time, then descend to the sands to go and flip an old gangster's evening on its head.

43.

We leave the beach and climb up the hill past a loose straggle of a few big houses. Sid's is the last one, Thomas says. The gate's open and there's no buzzer or bell to be seen, so we continue in and up the drive. There's a wide terrace looking west to the beach, the far mountains and the setting sun. On it sits a frail old man wrapped in a blanket for warmth.

It comes as one hell of a shock to realise this is my grandfather. In all the photos he's a muscled thug, gimlet eyes alive to all threat and opportunity. No more. He's turned inward and is near death.

"Oye! Es el propiedad privado!" is shouted from somewhere off to the side. The East End accent mangling the Spanish words is so pronounced that I almost laugh, but I can't take my eyes off the old man.

"Good evening Hawkins," says Thomas. "We need to speak to Sid urgently."

Of course. I've heard about Hawkins, the manservant who fancies himself a butler despite being from Bow Common. Sid did keep this little bit of the old country with him.

"Eh?...Mr. Thomas? But this is outrageous. You can't just turn up 'ere unannounced. Mr. Marsh ain't..."

"'Oo is it 'awkins?" The voice is a feeble croak, but it's still accustomed to being obeyed.

"It's that Mr. Thomas sir. 'Im wot 'elped with your book, if you remember? But 'e didn't call ahead or nothin'. 'Im and some young woman. They..."

"Thomas? Well I never! Come on up, come on up. Stop being such an old mother 'en 'awkins, for Gawd's sake."

Thomas walks up a concrete stair towards the terrace. I follow close behind him. Sid waves away Hawkins' attempts to help and levers himself upright with the aid of a stick. He nearly falls, but that's East End pride for you. It draws his focus to the ground, and so we're close by the time he looks up again and takes in my face.

"Bella?!" he wheezes in sudden agony. "Bella?!"

He's seeing a ghost. I WANT him to see her ghost.

I don't speak. This is for the oppressive arsehole you were Sid. This is for costing me my mother. You were a big part of what drove her from life before I was old enough to try and bring her back. This is for being such a violent demon that Danny didn't dare tell you about Bella's pregnancy because he believed you'd force her to terminate it and the number of weeks and whether she wanted to keep Terry's baby alive be damned. That's why you never knew you had a granddaughter: because you'd have killed me before I was born. And once they'd started down that road how could they ever turn round and tell you? You deserve every fucking millisecond of this.

I only relent when I start to worry his panic might kill him. We need the old bastard alive. "Wrong. I'm Cathy. Her daughter," I say tonelessly.

He collapses back into his seat.

"Oh Gawd," he gasps so faintly that it's barely audible. "Oh Gawd. Oh Jesus Gawd."

Hawkins flaps and fusses for an age. His every glance at us throws daggers, but he has the servant's terror of airing an opinion and seeing it not matter a jot. Finally he recognises that to continue not accepting Sid's claims he's fine will draw ire, and, defeated, he obeys the order to give us privacy.

Hunched up and tucked into his chair, Sid looks pitiful. I have no pity though. I don't trust myself. When I whisper "Please" to Thomas he understands that the story is needed without emotion.

"Danny and Bella were too scared of your reaction to tell you she was pregnant by Terry Norris. After Bella went Danny raised Cathy with Mrs. Canning and Eric, who I guess you know?"

Sid gives a faint nod.

"Some people are what I call ghosts. I'm one, so is Cathy, and so was Bella. It means your spirit can move outside your body, but there's a risk to it which is that it gets more and more painful to go back. When Danny was locked up and not there to keep giving her reasons to stay, Bella left her body for too long and her ghost faded away. That's how she died."

"Did you know?" I interject, my voice harsher than I want. I've wondered this for so long. I mean how could he not?

But Sid shakes his head. His hands are trembling beyond his control.

"Ghosts can't go on or in water," Thomas continues smoothly. "There's something about it that would tear us apart in an instant. Danny moved Cathy to his island as a way to keep her safe when she first started to leave her body like Bella had. He's devoted his life to protecting her."

Sid's mouth is opening and closing and making him look like some sort of stuck tortoise. I want to punch him, but Thomas' hand takes mine and his thumb gently massages a slower beat for my pulse. I squeeze back thanks when I'm there, and take over the story, as he wants.

"I won't call you grandad, Sid. I don't know how I feel about you. We're here because I want something from you."

That gets a new reaction from him. Weak as his body is, inside it is a mind with a lifelong wariness of anything other than taking.

"This...this can't be real. This ghost stuff...nah. It 'as to be all nonsense. What is it you're after Thomas? Money?"

I'm instantly livid again. Partly because addressing Thomas shows me just how fucking invisible women are to him, and partly at his ability to shrug clear of emotion that should have drowned him.

"By way of proof," Thomas slides in seamlessly. "One day after interviewing you I pretended to fall asleep in your garden. Actually I went in ghost form to your office. In there I found a receipt for a Smiths Imperial wristwatch inscribed 'World's Best Cleaner' and dated the morning after Norris and Hughes were blown up."

I've been meaning to ask him where he read that

inscription. Thomas and I really haven't had enough time to talk properly yet. "But not the morning after they died," I add matter-of-factly, having found some vein of ice in me to cling to. "That was a day earlier. And the murders weren't Danny's doing, were they?"

Sid's head goes into his hands and I wonder if he's weeping in self-pity, but when he removes them and looks up his eyes are dry and his face has remembered how to be hard.

"All of it were for Bella. All of it."

"Did you ever ask her if that was what she wanted?" I snap back.

The sun is touching the horizon outside and it turns him golden. "No," he admits at last. "So what is it you want then?"

"Danny," Thomas has a featherlight and calming touch, "left the pin of the grenade by the car the two men were in. The police found it and now Harry Hughes has a DNA match from it. There's a new law that removes the double jeopardy protection and he's going to use it to retry Danny for murder. Danny's likely to be put away for life."

"Fuckin' careless of 'im," Sid says finally.

"Yes," Thomas is in quickly before I can flame the old bastard. "It was. It hardly deserves a life sentence for a crime he didn't commit though. Nor should it cause Cathy to lose the man who's been a true father to her."

Sid blinks and then suddenly croaks out a vulture laugh. "Fuckin' 'ell. Did you two come all the way 'ere 'opin' I'd take the rap?"

Thomas nods. "We want you to tell the truth. Your confession will reduce the charges against Danny to not much more than the perverting the course of justice he's already served time for. I believe Hughes will do a deal for you and you alone."

"You know I'm dyin', don't you?"

"Yes," Thomas answers, now hard as any pirate king. "It's the only reason we had any hope you might agree."

"That's what you think of me? After all you wrote in my book?"

"It is. You've lived a self-serving life Sid. But you still have the chance to change its ending. Not everyone gets that."

Sid wheezes harder, his fists clench, but his body will no longer allow him resort to violence. I doubt he could even raise much of a shout. I watch the progress of his mind contort his face in the way of the elderly. It shifts, unaccustomed muscles, perhaps those for the expressions of softness and love, twitching into use. I start to feel a sliver of hope.

"Get the fuck off my property," he growls. "Now!" No-one moves. "'Awkins!"

Right away the butler is there, the flame of the low-ranking authorised to use aggression in his eyes. "You 'eard Mr. Marsh. Go on. Git! The both of you! Eh?!"

Thomas' hand is an iron manacle around mine, and it's just as well because I could and I would pummel the life out of that old fucker and his flunky too.

"Come on," he says impossibly calmly. "Goodbye Sid. Hawkins."

I'm so stunned I go with him meekly, and we're at the bottom of the road before I find my voice. "So that's that." It's not even a rhetorical question.

"I'm not sure."

"You what? You heard him."

"I didn't hear him say no."

"You're serious?" I jam the brakes on, making Thomas swing round to face me.

"Yes."

"He told us to fuck off."

"Or it was a crude way of asking for a little space and time to process all we'd just hit him with."

No-one, and I mean no-one, has ever been able to make my mist fade away once it turns red. Not until here and now, when Thomas makes me doubt. "Is this why you're so good at biography?" I mutter at him finally.

"If your own stories aren't strong enough you have to learn to read those of others."

All rage is gone now. "I'm sure your stories are good," I reassure my love.

"I'm sure they're not good enough, and that's completely fine. Come on. Hawkins is watching so let's keep moving. What he doesn't know is that we're coming back tomorrow, and the next day and the next day and the next day too if we need to."

I make my legs move and in a few minutes we're back on the twilit beach and walking west. The hills are silhouettes now, a layered colour chart of dark-blue-greens.

The tide has receded and we can pass round the headland. The surf foams to our right. The sky is orange here too, but an orange a world apart from London's.

As we draw near Espasante again Thomas asks if we should go and look for some food.

"No," I reply. "How many times do I have to raise the topic of sex with you before you get the hint?"

He stops dead.

"I believe you're right that there's hope for tomorrow," I explain, not looking at him. "It means all the pain that might be in the future isn't real yet. Ghosts need to seize such moments. Enjoy them."

He bends and plants a warm kiss on my lips, and then is off striding across the sand, pulling my hand so fast I have to run slightly to keep up with his long legs.

44.

We just keep looking at each other as we walk along the beach again. It was sensational. Then we left our bodies so our ghosts could merge, and back into them, and honestly it's all unclear because I was in such a state of delirious bliss. Oh life is so sweet. So amazingly sweet.

Sid has barely even crossed my mind all morning. I don't think Cathy's been able to dwell on it either.

"This is the place I've dreamt of," she says in morning-sunlit wonderment. "I didn't think it could exist, or if it did it was out of reach. But I'm here."

I slow, wanting to dally, but she pulls me onwards.

"We can come back anytime Thomas. We know it's here now. We know how to get here. But we have business to take care of."

I smile at how much she can sound like Danny, and we get to the road at the far side and walk up it.

There's no answer at Sid's house. We knock, try the gate, walk round it and listen. A dog takes up barking in the distance, but there's no other sound.

"Enjoy the view a moment," I tell her. "I'm just going to check inside."

We move a little further up the cliff path and lie down on the grass. She kisses me. "Come back to me soon."

Then I'm out of my body and through the wall into Sid's house. There's paperwork spread all over the dining room table but no sign of life. I go up and down, through all the bedrooms, into the basement, and back to the middle floor. Hawkins has a sad little servant's apartment on the lower floor. I don't think anyone goes upstairs at all, which is a waste because the view from the windows there is an absolute tonic for every single moment of every day. Sid's bedroom is at the back of the ground floor and is dominated by medical equipment for eking out the last scraps of life.

"No-one's home," I say when my body wakes.

"So," Cathy says, "we have some more time in limbo in paradise. How's your stamina, pirate king?"

It's this nickname she seems to have for me for some reason. I actually quite like it, at least so long as she doesn't want me to dress up in pantaloons and start saying yarrr and suchlike. "It's good. Shall we again?"

"Oh yes."

And it's actually better than yesterday if anything. We spend the evening the same way, after an afternoon walk along the beach reveals there's still no-one home at Sid's.

45.

Today when we go up the hill we're met by a very flustered Hawkins who is reluctant to open the gate. I grip Cathy's hand as I flush with sudden hope. If I'm honest I thought the chances were seventy-thirty against.

Sid is in his chair on the terrace, waiting. This time he's in control, just the way he likes it.

"See Thomas, I want to know if you've been honest with me."

"We have," I get in before Cathy can flare next to me.

"But this ghost bollocks...nah. Come on. Danny must have told you about that watch and you guessed there was a receipt."

Is this all that stands in our way? For a ghost it's no barrier at all. "May I?" I ask, already reaching down to the side table where there's pen and paper. I place them on Sid's blanketed knees and then walk to the far end of the terrace, Cathy following me with her eyes all lit up.

"Write any words you like on a piece of paper. Fold it to be sure I can't see it, and have Hawkins put it inside the house on the table. You'll be able to see my body the whole time. When I wake up I'll tell you what you wrote.

"Don't tire yourself sir," bleats Hawkins. "Let me. If you must go along with this 'ere nonsense."

But Sid waves him off. He looks at me and then he looks at Cathy, and his eyes are unreadable. Finally he bends forward and scrawls something on the paper behind a cupped hand. Folds it tight and gives it to Hawkins, who he commands: "Do it like 'e said. No fuckin' about."

I sit in a deckchair and leave my body. Briefly brushing Cathy's hand, I go past Sid and Hawkins and inside. The paper sits in the centre of the table, which is now cleared of other documents. Sid's writing is weak, and I suspect always was slightly childlike. I read it. Isn't it so, so East End of him that he needs to make me say these words rather than attempt them himself.

"I'm sorry Cathy," I say upon waking, and suddenly tears are streaming down Sid's old face.

"Alright then. I'll do it," says Sid, recovered enough and having shoved Hawkins away. "Jesus, can you do this ghost thing too Cathy? And Bella? I could 'ave been king of England! Medical ward or a jail'll near as make no difference to me now. Fact it'll be nice to 'ear English 'round me again. Bangers and mash for dinner. Get a paper I can read for a change."

It's Sid doing the necessary work on himself. I've always considered him perhaps the most selfish person I've ever met, and those walls can only crumble so fast and so far. I nod along as he explains in unnecessary detail why going back and facing the music is actually exactly what he wanted all along.

"But," suddenly his voice gains a businesslike edge, "wiv'

the little time I 'ave left Hughes ain't gonna accept my confession without a motive. I'll 'ave to say when and why I killed 'em. Bella's gone, Gawd rest 'er soul, but everyone's gonna know your story Cathy. Nastiest little shits the public schools can turn out runnin' them tabloids, an' they'll be making all their smart-arsed puns about you. Smut an' poison. You alright with being fed into that mill? You ready to face all that?"

I have the same question but have been deliberately shoving it aside.

"I'll cope."

"Even if they want a DNA match between you and Terry to prove Sid's testimony and it's in public evidence?" I add.

She holds her head high. "Yes." I'm not entirely convinced, but that's her answer.

Sid's less able to accept a woman's decision. "Well I don't like that. Not for me own flesh and blood. 'Ow long you two stayin' 'ere for?"

"We need to get back as soon as possible," I answer. "I have to talk to Hughes and get him to agree the deal before he moves on Danny."

"Right," rasps Sid. "We'll go to the notary in Ortigueira just before lunch today then. Get all the paperwork signed."

I frown, confused. "But Sid, you do understand you'll have to come back to London and confess in person? A sworn testimony from over here won't cut it."

"'Course not you plonker." His dry cackle is a ghost of the sly laugh when he caught me in some bit of naivety. "I mean to make this gaff over to Cathy. Got the deeds drawn up yesterday just in case. You'll need a place to get away from the bleedin' paparazzi won't you? I was watchin' you through the telescope when you walked 'ere, girl. Don't try and tell me you don't love this bit of the world. Go the other way from the 'ouse an' there's a place called Picon with the best view I ever seen in me life. Local bloke called Rafael wants to stick a park bench right on top of the cliff. I 'ope 'e never manages it. World might notice it's fuckin' paradise and then they'd all come 'an ruin it."

His chatter runs out.

"Go on," he pleads, gazing at his granddaughter. "I know it don't make everythin' right, but I've found me peace 'ere and I'd love this 'ouse to stay in the family. Not that I've a right to call you that, I know, but..."

"Sid," she cuts him off. "I won't return to live on Penitent's Isle. And I expect you're correct about being away from London for a while. You're also right that my forgiveness can't be bought. But I don't want to judge without hearing the truth, the whole truth and nothing but the truth. There's nowhere they can lock you up that I can't visit you as a ghost. I won't be able to speak, but I can move an object to let you know when I'm there. I'm prepared to listen to your side for as long as it takes. I want to. My answer's yes."

"Can't ask for fairer than that," Sid mumbles, sniffing.

For a moment I wonder if she'll go over and they'll embrace, but if their story could be ended so simply it would diminish it. Cathy's look is still hostile, and part of Sid's mind is already turning everything round to suit itself. But the situation is not without hope.

More practically, we have the agreement we came here to get, and I don't fear he'll renege on it. My task now is to work out how to make Hughes settle for the last few months of a dying man's life.

Because I fear mere truth may be no match for that policeman's need for vengeance.

46.

On the boat back to Penitent's Isle I again crouch down in the cabin. There's a little gap to peep through and I see the two rozzers take photos and leer nastily as we pass by. Everything is coming out into the open soon. It's show time. Show trial time. But whose?

Up ahead Danny and Mrs. Canning are waiting at the dock.

"How does it feel returning home?" Thomas asks me quietly.

"It's not home. My heart's not here. I'm not sure it ever was," I reply. The truth is I'm a mix of relieved Danny's not been taken yet, joyful that Thomas and I have each other, and unable to think clearly because honestly the air here reeks and I feel nauseous.

"How do you think Danny will take Sid giving you a house?"

"He'll be fine as long as he knows it doesn't mean much. It's just a thing."

Thomas raises an eyebrow. "We're talking about a luxury chalet. Nor do I believe it doesn't mean much to you, by the way. I might even get jealous if it wasn't you, because I think I'm in love with the place too."

"You are? And I mean it's Sid's giving it to me that doesn't mean much. The plus of being filthy rich is you can't be bought easily." It's an offhand reply and disingenuous; these last days have been an absolute whirlwind and it feels like something of a hangover coming on. "How are you doing?" I ask my ghost love.

"First we need to try and do the deal with Hughes, but that aside I'm absurdly excited about the future."

"And scared?"

"Do you know, no. But let's not go into anything too much

on this boat with all these smells. You're looking a touch green actually."

A thought suddenly occurs to me. "Why are we still going by boat? They can keep the drawbridge down now."

"I guess they might need the time it buys them to clean up before Hughes can get in."

That focuses me, and I deliberately breathe in a lungful of the stinking East End air. We've a job to do here.

It's the first time I've ever returned to Penitent's Isle not in crisis, so it's the first time I've ever been in a fit state to observe the deep, complicated love Danny has for me. I owe him so much, and I'm so glad I can finally give him something back. After hugs and handshakes the five of us make our way to the study.

"So?" Danny opens proceedings. He's looking at me but I'd rather Thomas deliver the report, so I turn to him.

"Sid agreed," he starts, causing three explosions of held breath. "The medical opinions give him four to six months. There are pills he can take that will give him a good couple of hours at the expense of a bad day or two after. He'll use those to make the trip back to Britain and to disguise his true condition from the papers and Hughes."

"And his cut? His terms? What does he want?" Danny demands. Something's eating him. It must be something he takes seriously to keep him angry in the face of the news we've brought.

"The chance to appease his ghosts via Cathy. Nothing else."

Danny turns to me. "I won't 'ave you selling yourself to 'im," he orders.

"I'm not," I reply firmly, and Mrs. Canning places a hand on Danny's arm and nods.

"I have carte blanche from him to negotiate with Hughes," Thomas continues defusingly. "We went through everyone else involved in the murders and they're all either dead or played such a small and hard-to-prosecute role that Hughes will trade them away. It's just you and Sid, and he's content for the whole truth, even about Bella, to be made public."

"As am I," I add.

"It'll be 'orrible," Danny says, suddenly so tender.

"Not as horrible as you being locked away for life. And Sid's provided me with a place to escape to. It's the best chance Danny, so we're doing it."

"I agree," says Mrs. Canning. "Well, well, well. Sid Marsh thinking of someone else. And Thomas here off to negotiate for the East Enders. Who'd have thought it. Do you have a specific plan Thomas?" she asks when everyone's settled again.

Now he's his wonderful mix of pirate king being deliberately self-effacing. "The sooner the better so I suggest tomorrow morning. Prep me this afternoon with the conditions and guarantees you want Mrs. Canning, and then any agreement will be draft pending your approval. I need to talk to Hughes in person, so that means going to Bow Road police station. I don't anticipate any problems or delays in getting in to see him. One more thing: I'd like Cathy there."

"Why?" Danny reacts like a guard dog. "The further clear of all this she is the better. No."

Eric fidgets awkwardly in the palpable tension. I bet he's wishing he'd stayed outside with his vegetables. But of course it's his home and his allotment on the line here too.

"I mean in ghost form. I appreciate your trusting me this way, but we're talking about all your futures. There's obviously no way I'm going to take along a tape recorder or anything, so I want her to be your witness there."

"Yes," I say clearly before anyone else can speak.

It's late before Thomas gets back to the cottage from Mrs. Canning's rooms. The bed's narrow and there's little space compared to the second floor, but no-one's made any comments about my moving in here. Mind you, they know I'd bite their head off if they did.

Thomas looks tired - almost as if he's been wandering - and preoccupied.

"All okay?" I ask.

"Just a lot of legalese. And a detail we had to confirm." He waves a hand to push it away, not wanting to go back into it now. "Mrs. Canning sees the law as a nest of traps, and explains why convincingly. I don't need to know all the specific clauses for tomorrow. She just wants to be sure I don't spoil the ground for when this comes down to documents."

We kiss and I massage his tense shoulders. In the silence we hear ships' engines out on the river. Later the small gate buzzes open, then there's the low hum of the launch going off.

I finally summon up the courage. "So," I say, perhaps more nervous than before the first time we met, "do you fancy some bedtime reading?"

In that instant, by his reaction, I'm aware of something my grandmother and mother never had: the man in their life keen to know and to nurture their talents. It's a different kind of electricity than when we touch, but every bit as good.

"Oh yes please," he breathes. And I hand him over the sheaf of paper.

"It's not finished yet. It's something new. Something I started writing the day you arrived here."

He places it carefully by the bed, and we change, clean teeth, and climb in under the duvet. I lie against him and wriggle down until my head's on his thigh, where I will myself to sleep. Then I leave my body and go to the foot of the bed to watch him read, biting my spectral nails. He's fast but thorough. The forty-two pages I have so far take him just over an hour.

"I think it's fantastic Cathy," he says aloud. "I wasn't aware I could admire you more, but this..."

And then he closes his eyes and soon his ghost rises from him. Words are stripped from us now, but as we merge all their good meanings are inside us and wonderful.

47.

"Thomas, Thomas, Thomas! I've been worried for you. Now what took you off to Spain in such a hurry?" says Hughes on the other end of the phone line.

"We need to meet," I reply, unsurprised that he knows. "This morning. I have information."

"My door is always open. When?"

"Eleven."

"I'll have someone waiting for you in reception. Looking forward to it Thomas."

I hang up and note that he didn't warn me about my flat being bugged, my phone being tapped or the possibility of my being followed. He thinks he's got me and has dispensed with the theatrics.

Cathy's body is in a small flat a street away that Danny acquired for the day. Her ghost is beside me as I reach the grand Edwardian police headquarters on Bow Road. The electricity of her touch tingles right through me.

"Don't make me look happy," I whisper, smiling.

Then I go inside and am recognised and led upstairs right away.

Hughes is all geniality. It masks his eagerness inadequately.

As we shake hands and I observe his face I'm confident he has no idea of what I'm about to reveal. We couldn't be certain, so that comes as a big relief.

"Well then, Thomas?" he asks once we're seated either side of a veneered desk.

"I can tell you who killed your brother and who killed Norris."

"You've found proof?!"

"Better. I can get you the full story in court under oath. Who, when, why and how. All of it."

He frowns the frown of someone who believes the only way is hard. "You're trying to tell me Danny Decker will confess?"

"That's not what I said. Your brother was murdered by Lawrence Tate, known locally as Larry the Lizard."

Hughes' face knots, eyelid twitching.

"As you probably know, Larry died in 1987. Everything he did was ordered by Sid Marsh. Sid killed Terry Norris himself. He did so because Terry raped his daughter, Bella."

"'Old on 'old on 'old on," shouts Hughes rising half to his feet and leaning forwards over the desk. "What is all this? I told you I've got the pin from the grenade that killed them - both of them in the same car at the same time - and that it has Decker's DNA on it. What are you going on about?"

I spread out my hands palms upwards. "It's the truth. Sid confirmed it."

"Ahhh! This all cooked up out in Spain was it? How did they turn you Thomas? Did they feed you such a good story that a hack writer like yourself couldn't resist, eh? Or is it money? Eh? Eh?"

I look at him calmly and quizzically, waiting. A fleck of foam forms at the corner of his mouth.

"I mean don't be fucking ridiculous sunshine. Sid was miles away in a packed restaurant. Don't you think I would of 'ad 'im years ago if he didn't 'ave a cast iron alibi, eh?"

"The time of the explosion was not the time of death of either man. The grenade was to hide the fact they'd both been dead since the day before."

Now he blinks, clears his throat, stutters a single syllable then runs dry. This is the key detail he never suspected. I feel sad watching it throw him so completely. Advancing age and unrequited obsession make unholy dance partners.

"Sid Marsh and Lawrence Tate are your murderers. That grenade was only obfuscation. Perverting the course of justice, if you prefer. Sid's prepared to confess."

Now he's suddenly furious, livid. "Don't fucking think I can be palmed off with the last dribble of a dying man's life. It's a con. I want Decker. I fucking want Decker."

"Danny Decker is not a murderer."

"I want the fucker anyway. I've waited too long. Someone 'as to pay a real price. They took my brother away. My kid brother."

"Bella had a daughter, Cathy. Your DNA technology and some exhumation or family tests can confirm she's Bella and Terry Norris' child. The rape is why Sid had him killed, not for grassing. He'd known for months what Norris was up to and had been using him to feed you misinformation."

"NO! I will NOT fucking accept this. You're trying to tell me this was all about Norris and Brian was killed just for cover? That he was nothing more than collateral fucking damage?! NO!"

"When you came to my apartment asking me to pass you information about Danny you talked about duty to society, law, justice and truth. I'm giving you the truth. Aren't you prepared to accept it and act upon it as your profession requires?"

"You fucking treacherous little smart-arsed fuck. Think the law's negotiable do you? Get the fuck out. Get the fuck out of my office and you better watch yourself too, boy. I've got enough without you. Yes, it's all lined up and I've got enough. Tell Decker no fucking deal and I'm coming for 'im. Now get out!"

I arrive back at the flat just as Cathy's coming round. Her eyes flicker open and seek mine, alarmed. She's about to speak but I hold up an apologetic hand, asking her to wait. Danny's face is unreadable. Mrs. Canning's eyes have the gleam of a hunter.

"He said no?" she asks.

"In very explicit language," I reply.

"And you explained new and relevant facts and evidence related to the case to him? Offered him sworn testimony?"

"Yes. Everything we discussed."

"You didn't identify Danny as handling the grenade?"

"No. Just referenced perversion of the course of justice to bring the double jeopardy rule into play as you wanted."

"And it's all on tape?"

I remove the slim Dictaphone from my inside pocket and hand it to her. "Yes."

"Then we've got the bastard," she says. "A press campaign or civil suit with this would remove any chance of convicting Danny." She's explaining this to Cathy, who's been listening in a mix of surprise and confusion. "But the powers that be will never let it get near that. They're not going to have the first use of their shiny new law shot down in public."

"Where's Eric?" Cathy asks suddenly.

"Out on 'is ear and watchin' 'is back if 'e knows what's good for 'im," snarls Danny, finally able to vent about this.

"I'm sorry Cathy," I say. "Eric was passing information to Hughes."

"What?" she gasps.

Mrs. Canning snorts. "Took your storyteller here to connect the dots. Danny and I had been racking our brains how Hughes could have found out Thomas was coming to Penitent's Isle in advance. We were down to four names. Then Thomas texted on the way to the airport asking me to...how did you phrase it? Make sure Eric didn't learn that the world's best cleaning took place the following day. We didn't want to believe it could be our groundsman, but without that piece of knowledge Eric would assume Sid's confession related just to ordering the killings. When you got back and Thomas came to my office he left his body there and went in spook form to Eric's cottage to check."

I take over. "I'm so sorry I couldn't tell you. I didn't know how you'd react you see. I wasn't sure either. It only occurred to me on the morning we went to Spain, but I thought it was plausible and I saw a way we could turn it round if it was true. And then every single thing we'd said in Eric's hearing - apart from all the ghost stuff that is; I guess he didn't want to sound crazy to Hughes - was noted down on bits of paper tucked behind the drawer of his dresser, ready to hand over on his next boat trip."

My love finally sighs. "His memory never was much good," she says sadly.

"I sent Eric off to shore on an errand that same evening," continues Mrs. Canning gleefully. "When I checked his dresser and the notes were gone it meant we knew what Hughes believed. That he'd assume our ask was going to be a lighter sentence for Danny for turning crown witness to Sid ordering the killings. But he had no idea about when the murders really happened and that Danny didn't kill either man.

"That meant he would have no suspicions about agreeing to meet Thomas. And he would swallow that clever detail about

Thomas not taping the meeting, and speak freely. Then, whether he said yes to our actual deal or refused it to pursue his vendetta, the simple fact of his hearing out the truth and us recording it gave us the win.”

“Can you forgive me for not telling you and making you go through this charade?” I ask.

“It was my request,” adds Mrs. Canning firmly. “You wear your heart on your sleeve Cathy, and you’ve known Eric all your life. I couldn’t risk that he might notice a change in you.”

Cathy purses her lips and then nods. “You made the right call. Thank you for doing it the way you did. I’m not sure I could have hidden that from him.”

Danny, who’s been fidgeting more and more, growls again, but Mrs. Canning wags a finger at him. “He must have had a very good reason to do it Danny. No retribution, at least until we understand.”

Cathy nods agreement, and although Danny looks like he wants to spit on something then strangulate it, he finally relents and mutters “Okay”.

“What next then?” I ask to move things along.

“Now I go to get a signed agreement that gives them the truth, Sid, and no-one else,” says Mrs. Canning.

“You’re going to visit Hughes?” I ask, struggling to envisage the old inspector ever seeing reason.

“’Course not. His superior in the echelons of the Met.”

“Can you really arrange that kind of appointment?”

“Happens we’ve got leverage. Some photos of the Assistant Commissioner in question having his fun to cash in. Told you it was all just a nasty game, didn’t I?”

48.

Three weeks ago to the day a writer came to join us on

Penitent's Isle. Now I wake next to him on his uncomfortable West London bed which is also a sofa.

I don't want to be here.

I want our bodies entwined and this physical world, of course. The colour is bright in it now, and is here to stay. I just want to be in that house in Espasante instead. I want to look out on cliffs and sand and sky rather than the wall across the street. I want to hear the ocean's mood to start my day, not car engines and frustrated clamour. I'm deeply ashamed of the thought, but I can't wait for Sid to move out so I can move in.

Thomas is sound asleep. He got up to write at five and only came back to bed at seven-thirty. His computer screen's blank so I don't know what he worked on. I will buy him a typewriter. I'd like to begin my mornings reading the words that came to him in the night.

For now I make him coffee, a drug to which he's already a shameless slave at thirty. He wakes and gives me a beaming smile from beneath dishevelled hair.

We potter for half an hour, although this space is woefully inadequate for pottering.

"Do you genuinely think it's necessary to live in London to be a writer?" I ask him in a fit of irritation as I fight the bed-sofa into its upright position.

He considers this. "I suppose it depends to what extent you're writing for other people or yourself."

"Good answer," I reply. "Or perhaps it's a good question. Was your pre-dawn typing more notes for Danny's autobiography?"

"It was."

"And do you think that will happen now?"

"I've no idea. I was planning to ask you."

"The original reasons for it no longer stand, certainly."

His shoulders slump slightly. "I know. On that note, should

we get going? Penitent's Isle awaits our presence."

After an enjoyable weekend away in this disappointing side of the city I'm returning to my former home this morning. But home is now wherever my kindred spirit is.

Although we do need a bigger place to haunt than this miserable bedsit of his.

The house in Espasante for example.

Do you know what I love? I used to dread the future. Now I'm just ravenously impatient for every day.

The taxi drops us at the car park where Hughes' men aren't anymore. Only the remains of a dropped takeaway that's been mostly devoured by seagulls testifies to their presence. I wonder if that happened the evening Thomas was trapped outside? As we walk by the place I still have where his ghost lay marked exactly.

"I wish it had been somewhere more romantic than a marsh next to a landfill," he says, our thoughts in sync as seems wonderfully always to be the case. I laugh and we walk on hand-in-hand to the drawbridge, which is down.

Mrs. Canning is bringing us up to date. Sid will fly over next week to deliver himself into custody at the airport. It will be a whole great show of law and sternness and uniforms with even the Home Secretary getting in on the grandstanding. The trial will be as fast as it is unnecessary, because the last thing they want is for the star turn to die before justice can be done to him. The general thinking is that if he can survive at least a month after conviction the tabloids will have moved on and everyone can congratulate themselves. Hughes will be kept as far away from the proceedings as possible. He's not a reliable actor.

Now she turns to me. "Think carefully about what you will do Cathy. You and Thomas. I didn't even float the idea of removing Bella's rape from evidence. They would have argued that it's vital to show motive and I would have lost an ask. We all know that sex sells newspapers, all the more so the nastier it is and the prettier the girl involved. There will be photos of your mother on every front page. You're going to have the paparazzi after you. You've got ten days or so, after which I'd advise you to either hole up here or get out of the country altogether."

"Thomas and I will go to the house in Spain," I announce. I asked him this in a particularly filthy tube carriage during zone three of the Docklands Light Railway - I figured I was owed a little manipulation for being kept in the dark about Eric. He said yes with alacrity.

"But," and here is the bit he doesn't know and wouldn't be sure about. I am though. "In the time we have left we'll stay here so Thomas can get the rest of the details he needs for Danny's autobiography."

Thomas looks at me with an eloquently raised eyebrow.

"I don't think that'll happen now," says Danny.

"It could still play well," counters Mrs. Canning. "I don't trust the Metropolitan police force as far as I could throw them. You remain a target Danny. For any upwardly mobile inspector looking to prove themselves. I mean Sid only did 'As Nails' to guard against extradition proceedings, and look how well it worked."

"But not just the whole hard-case macho-bravado thing," I continue as if no-one's spoken at all. "The truth. Enough of it's going to come out in the trial anyway, so why not own the narrative? Why not let the world also see what a loving, devoted, decent man you are despite all the pain fate has thrown at you and those long, long, East End odds against?"

Danny seems lost for words. Then, unbelievably, he begins to cry, and what starts as a trickle is soon a flood. "You tell no-one about this," he rasps, more embarrassed than I've ever seen him, but unable to stop.

"Or we tell everyone," puts in Thomas gently. "Because this is the hidden half of your real and poignant story. I, at least, respect and admire it infinitely more than any fiction."

"You still want to write it do you?" Danny fires at him hotly as he struggles to regain self-control.

"I do," says my wonderful love calmly.

There's a long pause. "No. No autobiography." The finality in Danny's answer shocks everyone into silence. "But if you really want to do this then I'll agree to an authorised biography. Your name on the cover."

I can only run to Danny and hug him as tight as my arms will allow me because, as he always has, he's made everything as perfect as he can for me. When I finally release him I look around. Thomas is smiling appropriately, but the pirate king light shines from his eyes.

"I'll have to write Cathy's seclusion as hiding her from Sid and gangland politics in general," he says. "Maybe hint at trauma and recovery from it, etcetera. The world at large isn't ready for our actual type of ghost. It's not ideal, but it's far better than how the tabloids will paint things." He looks at me in question and I nod. I quite like the idea of dictating my warped story. Also, I'm a little ashamed to say, the cynical advantages I'm aware it might bring. I meet Danny's gaze, and even if there are some deep scars in there, he's unwavering in his new support of all my choices.

Mrs. Canning, however, seems discontent.

"Oh the biography idea plays beautifully and Thomas will do it well," she says dismissively, sensing my questioning look.

"It's not that. Danny, I want you to take Eric back."

"You what?!"

Way to make that lovely moment last, I think, but refrain from saying out loud.

"You want me to take a grass back into my home? No way."

"What have I ever asked you for before?"

"Nothing," he admits. "But why this? It's breaking the code. I'll lose face."

"Aren't you strong enough to do that?"

Thomas and I stand like rabbits in the headlights as the hard gangland boss and his apparently harder lawyer-stroke-housekeeper glare at each other.

"It's not a question of strength. It's just wrong."

"No. Wrong is that Eric's younger sister's got a head-in-the-clouds boy that she dotes on and fifteen months ago you fixed him up with some jobs to pay off his debts."

"I must be misunderstanding you here, Elsie, because it seems you're chucking that bit of charity back in my face."

"You're bloody well right I am. Did you ever meet Eric's nephew?" It's a cross-examination and I wouldn't be in Danny's shoes right now.

"No," he admits. "Wasn't any need to."

"So you figured help the family out with some fast cash and by the sound of things it'd do no harm to harden the boy up a bit at the same time?"

Danny draws himself upright. "More or less. What of it?"

"Details, research and strategy Danny!" Mrs. Canning shouts exasperatedly. "It's why you owe half your empire to me. Details, research and strategy. That boy's slender as a willow and looks like some beautiful elf. His debts came from drama school, which his dad wouldn't give him a penny towards because he didn't want his son to turn into a pansy. I went to see him in a play. He's actually pretty good. Beyond useless as an enforcer though. But what your blundering did achieve was a chance for Hughes to blackmail himself an informant. He targeted that kid and built a dossier. Minor nothings all of it, but make it suggest 'bad apple' and the right judge would have sent him down for a year or two. Know what they'd do to a boy like that in prison do you Danny?"

"Yeah," he admits sheepishly after a pause.

"So did Eric and so did Hughes. The first ask would have seemed harmless. Probably the second and the third too. Eric wouldn't tell me exactly how that copper played him but..."

"You went to see him?!"

"Obviously. He blubbed every bit as much as you did just now, so ashamed he was. It barely even helped telling him I'll make sure the file on his nephew gets erased as a condition of the deal for Sid. Oh for God's sake Danny, just let him come home. What he did actually worked out perfectly for us."

Danny frowns and blinks and twitches as he swims into unfamiliar waters. "Why didn't he say something?"

"Because he's Eric! The man gets by on about a dozen words per year."

"I don't know."

"Don't you make me threaten to leave you Danny Decker. I want Eric back. If nothing else I need him for his fresh veg."

I giggle at the double entendre. I try not to but I can't help it.

"Oh alright then," says Danny after a choice couple of swear words.

Mrs. Canning nods and then swivels her sniper gaze onto me. "And as for your question, no, there's never been anything like that between me and Eric."

How did she know I've always wondered that?

"Because I can good as read minds," she says.

Are you a ghost too? I think. Have you been able to see

every thought in my head the whole time?

This she either doesn't perceive or chooses not to answer.

"Elsie Eelsworth was the first in her whole family to stay in school past fifteen," she says instead, her eyes now faraway. "At eighteen I started working as a secretary, but two years later, in 1962, the new maintenance grant meant anyone could go to university. All you needed was a brain. I got my law degree with first-class honours and I knew I wanted to go for the bar, but the problem was I was single, working-class, and - if I say so myself - an attractive young woman. It would have been an absolute bloody nightmare of harassment and proposals and secret poetry and stalking and offence taken and well-connected vendettas I wouldn't have survived. Thus in the summer of my twenty-fourth year I married Mr. Canning, and he's been the best husband I could have wished for."

"Because he was a phantom?" Thomas looks delighted by the sheer invention at play here.

"Mr. Canning gave me everything I ever wanted from a man. Also, Eelsworth? How did such an awful surname ever come into existence? Was one of my ancestors once worth the same as an eel? So I took the name of the place I was born instead."

I look at Danny and see he's known all of this all along. I don't begrudge him this secret though. It wasn't his to share. When it comes down to it I respect a good confidence-keeper more.

"Could Elsie Eelsworth and all she did go in my book?" Thomas asks.

"Hmmm."

"I did agree to take Eric back," Danny puts in, raising his hands when she shoots a glare at him.

"Why not. Doesn't affect my ability to scrub a floor or cook the dinner, does it?" Mrs. Canning says at last.

Epilogue

Seven months later.

Cathy wakes beside me in our prison-view rented house in Woolwich. She looks tired. I guess it's been a long night, so I wait until she's ready to begin talking about it.

"Sid doesn't have long left. He held off upping the morphine because he wanted to be alert for this visit, but he needs it because he's in a lot of pain."

I wriggle an arm below her neck and hug her. She's warmed to her grandfather more than she expected these last fifteen weeks. The staff in the medical wing think he's lost his marbles, given the way he spends half his nights talking to the empty air.

"The strange thing was I think he could almost see me this time. He knew I was there before I gave him the sign."

"And what did he say? Anything new?"

"No, but the way he repeats things has mellowed. It still tickles him that they called the place Belmarsh after his daughter, as he enjoys wrongly insisting. He's seen a few more old friends and some old enemies in the last couple of days. Apparently once they're sure you're about to die the normal rules get suspended. It's funny to think of all these withered old hard-cases giving and receiving apologies and explaining themselves in search of closure, but by Sid's account that's what's going on. It seems to be a right soap opera in there in fact. The window near his bed's got a sliver of view to the river and the East End beyond it. We said our goodbyes. I won't return."

Gentle tears are spilling down her cheeks and I kiss her in sympathy.

"It's okay. He doesn't want me to see him gone and gaga."

"And his spirit? You're not curious to see if it emerges?"

"No. This is how I prefer things. I believe he's done with

the world, so I doubt there'll be so much as a flicker of anything. Even if there is a beyond for him I wouldn't want to hold him up or distract him; he's got his apologies all rehearsed in case Bella and Laoise are waiting for him. I kind of hope they are and that he gets his second chance. I also hope they're not and that they haven't even bothered to leave him a note."

"So it's just wait and then deal with the practicalities?"

"Yes. Not that there are many. Hawkins is the executor and over the moon to get the house in Bethnal Green, which is all there really is in the will. He visited yesterday and spent the entire time grumbling at Sid; hated the food in Spain; didn't trust the people; found Spanish too loud and harsh; too hot there; rained too much; couldn't get the papers or a proper Sunday roast. I reckon Sid will be glad to die before the man's due again. There's a little box of old photos and nicknacks earmarked for me, but that can be posted."

I sit up eagerly. "Does that mean we can go? I've been running out of excuses to avoid people who want to be earnest at me over literary lunches. I really want to be back home."

"Me too. But we have this morning's meeting first, remember? Speaking of which, if we leave right away we can fit in a Panamanian Geisha at Mork & Stark first."

I laugh, but rather wistfully. "Not likely. It's impossible to get a table there these days." People, it turns out, do like a good thing after all. And will shamelessly crowd out those who noticed it first. "It's all these new...what did you call them and all their facial hair?"

"Hipsters. I know you're older, but don't be turning into a curmudgeon on me yet Thomas Harrison! Anyway that Elin has a crush on you so if you call ahead they'll save a spot for us. Please do so in fact, because I'm in need of the good stuff to wake up properly. Today could really matter."

❖

I'm expecting Tarquin to come bounding down to reception in the Pevensey Literary Agency. I am currently their third-highest earner after all. He's looking awkward and hangdog though. I'm not sure why; no-one ever has bad news to give me anymore.

Then I spot Tarquin senior and Robyn Brookes following behind him, all dazzling smiles.

"Thomas! The gorgeous and also talented Cathy!" booms senior.

"We're honoured!" gushes The Witch.

I tilt my head at them in question.

"Well you're hot property Thomas," she says, rubbing her hands together. "We've got movie stars, retired politicians and even, wait for it - drum roll - a royal just lining up! They're all desperate, and I mean simply desperate, for you to do for them what you did for Danny Decker."

"So?"

"This is the major league Thomas. It's not a place for amateurs now is it?"

By the way my friend Tarquin junior cringes I'm left in no doubt who is being referred to. I point at him. "The contract I signed specifies that he is my agent, correct?"

"Well, yes. But the agency..."

"Then if he requires any support from you I trust he'll let you know. Now if you don't mind I have a busy morning."

I don't regard myself as a vengeful man, but I greatly enjoy it as I stand there watching them splutter their 'Of course's and 'Never any intention's as part of an awkward and platitude-flecked retreat.

"My pirate king!" Cathy laughs.

"Jesus Tom!" says Tarquin, trying not to look gratifyingly exultant. "And thank you. You don't know what it means to...Well. Ahem. What's happened to you these last months?"

I grin. "Maybe the East End rubbed off on me. That or success has given me a whacking great bat and sometimes I enjoy using it. Are any of these offers someone I'd want to write?"

Tarquin exhales himself calm. "Possibly. Don't for pity's sake go near the royal. Plays at our club. Thinks he's God's gift but I seriously doubt the man can manage his own shoelaces. It would drive you up the wall. There's a summary of what's on the table with a few notes from our meetings with them. Peruse it and we'll talk, but if there's nothing that grabs you then there's no rush. Your star's good for some time yet. But anyway, in here and we can get on to the real agenda for today."

We follow him into the plush meeting room with the view. Cathy's hand worms into mine. It's trembling. "So?" she squeaks.

Tarquin turns and then bows to her. "It's one of the best early drafts of a debut novel I've ever read."

I would say something to cover the emotions getting the better of her, were I not in the same state. I always thought this, but there's nothing like independent verification to make you believe talent's real.

"It's not the finished article though," Tarquin continues with a defusing smile. "And whilst I detect Tom's polish at work he's not the right editor for you."

"You don't mind?" she asks me.

"Oh no. I agree one hundred percent."

"I've got a couple of names. They'll bring the old-hand publishing experience you need. They're expecting your call but take your time with the choice and don't make it unless you're convinced. You're looking to be challenged without being changed. To keep raw but smooth out rough. A good editor shows you the path but never tries to walk it for you."

"Did you rehearse all that?" I ask him.

"Surprisingly, no."

"You really think people will want to read it?" Cathy asks. "To me it just feels so inadequate and unstructured and over-wordy."

Tarquin grins. "Show me a self-confident novelist and I'll show you a bad one. I actually devoured the whole thing in a single sitting until five in the morning. Slept in and missed an important meeting the next day. You're the genuine article Cathy, no doubt in my mind."

After Sid flew in we flew out, and disappeared into our own bubble for the next three months. We each set up in a different corner of the upper floor, me with my neat laptop and her with her dreadful clacking typewriter and piles of annotated paper everywhere. We lost track of the days of the week and time altogether. Occasionally we would walk the beach to Espasante and find everything except the bars closed because it was unexpectedly Sunday.

My biography of Danny was constructed. Her novel grew organically. In the evenings we would stop being writers and become each other's readers. It was magical. By the time the real world reeled us back in we'd lost every perspective on everything else and were no longer even sure that what either of us had was publishable. Now that I'm quite famous and she's surely going to be, I'm not certain we'll ever enjoy such a period of purity again.

My book was rushed out soon after the trial and I got my adulation fix quicker. She's going to get more though. She'll also be remembered a hundred years from now, whereas I doubt I will be. Or perhaps just as a hyperlink - I believe they're calling them - on her page of the internet encyclopaediae that will apparently contain all human knowledge then: Cathy's husband was Thomas Harrison, the noted biographer.

...who achieved early infamy when, under a pseudonym, he

entered and won the... There'll never be any exorcising that, will there!

"I have a small confession to make." Tarquin knocks me out of my reverie. "I took a teensy liberty and exceeded my brief rather and, well, talked to a couple of publishers."

Cathy gasps. "It's not ready."

"It's a lot more ready than you imagine. Also the lead time for an imprint is pushing on a year, and...well, as your agent my advice has to be that it's best to be pragmatic about the leverage your current place in the nation's consciousness acquires while it remains fresh."

"And?" I ask, once I've unscrambled his sentence. I glance at Cathy and I'm fairly sure she was already fully aware of this. Quite the pirate queen herself, it seems!

By way of reply to my question, Tarquin rustles amongst papers and passes Cathy a draft contract. "They liked it."

She scans it, jumps, and then passes it to me with a rather terrorised smile. "Is this...? Well... Your thoughts please."

A publishing contract of any form is the stuff of a million scribbler's dreams. This one's weighty. I brush past disclaimers and an NDA. "What?!"

Tarquin beams. "Yep!"

"A fifty thousand advance on a debut fiction novel?!" I pause and channel my new inner East Ender. "Although if they're prepared to offer this then there's more you could squeeze out...but no. If you're after my opinion, it's better to have a shot at earning out if you want a long career."

"Which I do."

She's just achieved the dream I've held in my heart from age thirteen. I'm so happy for her I could burst.

"Can I take this and have a friend look it over?"

Mrs. Canning. I pity the poor publisher.

"Absolutely," says Tarquin. "I should tell you there was

another offer for a bit more money. I'd recommend this one though. Long term they're more who you'd want to be with. For example the other party wanted to change the title. Felt yours was a bit un-literary and would cramp your chances at the flashier prizes."

"No then," says Cathy so firmly it reminds me of the man who brought her up. "This book has always had its name. It's called 'Ghosts'."

The End

Acknowledgments

This book is dedicated to my dad, Mike Imrie, who sadly never got to read it. I believe he would have enjoyed it.

Thus this one's first reader was my mum, Denise Imrie, who made it very clear how very much she enjoyed it. That truly meant a lot.

My wife Anna Dahlberg, my wonderful partner in life and now in making books, didn't read this until we got the proof copy. Thank heavens, she enjoyed it!

Likewise we hope our boys, Daniel and Otto, will when they're old enough. For all that being parents has its challenges, these two make us proud and bring joy to our lives every day.

A handful of good friends and fellow authors read early drafts of Ghosts. Enjoyment was little more than a footnote as they told me in detail everything they felt was wrong with it. These were my test readers, and I'm so grateful for their honesty and their ability to see the wood for the trees.

And now you are this book's newest reader, for which thank you, and I sincerely hope some enjoyment came your way through these pages.

If it lingers still, reviews and recommendations make my books stand out from the (vast) crowd, and so really do help a self-published author like me keep writing.

Similarly posts, reposts, tweets, likes, follows and so forth. Essentially, if you feel positively about this book then it'd be marvellous if you can let others know.

About the author

David Imrie was born in Oxford, England, in 1973. During his childhood his family moved first to Dorset and then to Thurso in Caithness, where he lived between ages 10 and 18.

He read psychology at Oxford University, an arbitrary choice of subject made hastily at 17 and perhaps something of a pattern. After a few years in psychiatry research and Manchester, David stumbled into IT in search of a way out. He ended up in software integration and error management, and for 3 months in 2005 knew of a simple way to kill every Nokia Series 40 colour phone in the world.

David's (very 2000s) plan behind returning to university to study architectural technology was to set up in Galicia, northern Spain, restoring old farmhouses for foreign buyers. Then Brexit nobbled that whole idea.

In 2017, getting kind of desperate, David asked a publisher acquaintance if he needed any proof reading doing. "If you want, but it's awfully dull stuff," came the reply. "Why not give editing a bash?" So he did, and it was a fit. Soon, of course, he started itching to do a bit of writing himself... Ghosts is his second novel.

David lives with his wife Anna and their two sons near the Galician town of Pontedeume. On lucky days he spots dolphins from his study window.

Also by David Imrie

The Lost Piece (Divers Novels, 2024) is available from most booksellers in paperback and eBook.

Joel just wants to qualify as an architect and get free from the gnawing pressure of student debt. This seems a distant dream, until he steals a bejewelled square of elaborate ironwood from an unearthed corpse.

In the far north of Scotland, local veterinarian Nat possesses an heirloom from her Russian aristocrat ancestor: a beautifully-crafted jigsaw puzzle missing its centre.

Combine their pieces and the two can share a quarter-million-pound windfall. But completing the puzzle fulfils another purpose. Something from the worst depths of the occult.

Paradice will be released by Divers Novels in spring 2025.

In a rapidly-heating world, what could be a more perfect find than a cut-price dream cottage in the Scottish Highlands?

But what if its seller knew something was about to go into reverse? The AMOC current underpinning the Gulf Stream, source of Northern Europe's temperate climate.

Already the seasons are turning and the ice is building. When winter arrives Marianne, Charlie and their unborn baby's new life will turn into a battle for survival.

Find out more at **davidimrie.com**